G000065603

'The Revival'

by

Michael Dennis

Book One in 'The Bringer of Shadows' Trilogy

This novel is entirely a work of fiction. The names, characters and incidents portrayed in it are work of the author's imagination. Any resemblance to actual persons, living or dead is entirely coincidental.

Copyright © Michael Dennis 2019

All rights reserved. Michael Dennis asserts the moral right to be identified as the author of this work. No portion of this book may be reproduced in any form without permission from the author.

Follow me on Twitter;
@authorMDennis

Tweet about the book using the hashtag #bringerofshadows

and for my latest blog updates, visit my author page on Goodreads;
Michael Dennis

About the Author

Born in Nottinghamshire, Michael Dennis studied History at University before moving to the city of Newcastle. He has been an avid reader of fantasy from a young age, listing Roald Dahl, Stephen King and C.S Lewis amongst his favourite authors.

Having written stories for his family during his childhood, Michael made it his New Year's resolution back in 2017 to write a fully-fledged novel. After two years of planning, research and rewrites, he has now finished the first of a planned trilogy entitled 'The Bringer of Shadows.'

Acknowledgements

I would firstly like to thank my Mum and Dad for their constant support and being such great parents. Also, thanks to my brother Gareth, my sister-in-law Flick and my nephew Finley. Finley, I'm very much looking forward to spending time with you and seeing you grow over the next few years!

I would also like to thank my Grandma Maureen and my best friend Emma. Like me, they are both big lovers of fantasy. I hope you both enjoy reading my first book as much as I enjoyed writing it!

Helen Creswell, author of over a hundred children's stories in her life, inspired me to write when I was a young lad growing up in Nottinghamshire. Also, thanks to Stephen Spinks, my former manager at Packwood House for his invaluable advice when starting this book.

Finally, a big thank you to Amazon KDP, who give a platform for independent authors like myself to publish their work and share their stories with the world.

Map of Northern Terra, the continent in which 'The Revival' is set in

MORODIR MOUNTAINS

The Shimmering Isle

The Dwarven Kingdom of Kahr Dovidor

The Circle Tower

The Monastery

The Cave

Port Isaak

The Haunted Forest

NORR

Northwood Academy

Tulusa

Jarlstadt

Durgan Marshes

Godeburg Academy & Town

Reno

Northwood Town

NULRASSA

FOCEA

Sleima

The Elven Kingdom of Usthyr

AKIRA REGION

Akira

Los Reyes

'The Revival'

One

In a deep sinister cave at the edge of the world, a great evil was reborn. It was an evil that had been considered so horrific by those in power that its mere existence had been wiped from the pages of history in the sheer hope that the next generations would never learn of the horrors that it possessed, or had been willing to use. The evil in question once had a name, which to an outsider had been as innocuous as a mere whisper in the wind; 'Leona.' Those who had been unlucky enough to cross her path, or the small faction that had been charged in bringing her down knew her simply as 'The Sorceress.'

For one man, bringing her back to life meant everything to him. He had sacrificed so much to get to this point, leaving behind a loving family and a large group of friends, as well as disavowing a well-respected military role that had brought him to this very cave. And so he had remained all of these years, biding his time, meeting informants and wealthy aristocrats, building up a military force on a scale the world had never seen before, all on the promise of utilising a great power that would bring eternal prosperity to Focea, his homeland. Its empire had been once the largest and most envious of all, brought down in a shower of fire and blood. It broke the man's heart to think what the region once was and what it had turned into, ruled by a group of petty lords squabbling over township matters. Focea needed to be unified under one ruler with one direction.

And he knew he was that man.

He knelt at the edge of the pool, its glowing pink waters on a level with the backwalls that gave it the illusion of stretching out eternally. He cupped both hands into it and brought a palmful of water up to his parched mouth. The pool was renowned for its healing qualities and so, as it travelled down his throat and into his stomach, he felt instantly rejuvenated, ready for what was about to happen.

"Not long now, my lady," he whispered to the bloodless, shrivelled corpse laid out at the bottom of the waters from where it had fallen twenty five previously, his hand stroking what remained of her scalp. "The day I have dreamt of has now arrived. You will awaken once more and together we will rule for eternity."

The man heard the three witches come before he saw them. Night had fallen outside and for a brief moment beforehand, he had wondered if he had been tricked. One by one they came down the zigzagging path, their bare feet scraping hard on the gravel, carrying nothing but the filthy rags they were dressed in. To him, their images were blurred, as if he were looking through a camera out of focus, appearing somewhat translucent.

"You're late," he said from the shadows, irritated by having to have waited so long, his frustration palpable in his sharp tone.

"One is never late," spoke back the eldest witch. "Our timing is always perfect." She then regarded the man's strange attire with a questionable look. "It is you that is in a hurry."

He looked fit to burst, but remained silent. Inside, his mind was racing; *'Of course I'm in a hurry! I have so much riding on her revival. I have made promises to men I have to keep, taken money from their coffers all in the vain hope of leading an army into battle. If the plan fails, then it all will have been for nothing and I will be an outlaw for ever more.'*

"We understand your little predicament," she replied, reading his mind as all good witches were prone to do. "That is why you came into our forest and knelt before our hut, begging for our help. We are your last hope. Am I right?"

The witch had the truth of it. The man had tried literally everything to bring her back to life; first of all, he had nearly bled himself dry, blanketing the waters in a deep scarlet. When that failed, he had gathered back his strength and travelled to a nearby village, offering a pair of goats to the Sorceress as a sacrifice, using a ritual he had learnt from a sacred text. Still in death's grasp she remained, her body slowly rotting on the riverbed. He had tried the same method with men, women and children until there was nobody left to capture and kill. Before the man slit the village elder's throat, he had spoken of three sisters that lived in a haunted forest on the other side of the continent of Terra. Of course, the man was wise to the ways of the world; he was well aware of the foul creatures that resided there and that if he were to bend the knee and require their help, they would demand something in exchange. Yet, asked them he had, preparing to offer them money. They had each cackled to his face, performing a merry dance in front of his very eyes.

'What use is money to us?' they had scalded him. Instead, they had demanded the ownership of his soul. He knew that would mean he would be under their control, but the honest truth was that he was fast running out of options.

"Sisters, let us commence with the witches rune and bring this corpse back to the earth from which she was born from."

"Aye, sister," said the second. From what the man could tell, this one was fatter than the rest and her face was obscured with some kind of strange basket-mask.

"Tis time," then returned the third, her body resembling the shape of a chicken, cackling to herself, her voice much shriller than the other two.

"Do I need to do anything?" asked the man.

The first witch began to chuckle. "We require nothing from you but your soul." A grave severity then gripped her voice, the next question simply stunning him. "Are you sure you want this to happen?"

He spun his head around just to make sure the crone had been addressing him rather than her 'sisters.' Why in God's name had she asked that? Of course he wanted this to happen. The reality was that he had gone way too to turn back now. "Why would you ask me such a strange question?"

"Because you must understand what we are about to unleash on the world. Once we start, young sir, then there is no going back."

"I am more than prepared to face the consequences."

"Hmm, are you though?"

Was he prepared? Did he actually know what he was involving himself with? Black magic, it was known as in some circles. He nodded repeatedly, removing the doubt from his head as quickly as it had entered. "Of course I am."

The first then cut in, moving closer to him. "You never said your name when you crossed into our realm."

He hesitated and then said, "Salt. My name is Rufus Salt. But I'm sure you know that already."

"And what do you hope to become, Rufus Salt?"

He wondered what the witch was trying to get at. Before, he had been nothing more than a middling rank soldier in the Akiran militia. But that was then and this was now. "I will become the Captain of the Focean army," he said, confidently. "Books will be written about me. I will be talked about for centuries. I will become the greatest soldier that has ever lived."

With a wicked leer, the witch stepped boldly into the clearing and whispered something to her sisters. "You have ambition, Rufus Salt," she said after a moment. "We like that."

Therein began the witches rune, which became a repeated chant that lasted no more than five minutes, each sister generating a wailed excitement, shrieking together extrovertedly exaggerated voices that resembled the strangling of a pack of cats. The heat became unbearable and then, out of nowhere, a maelstrom of wind hit the man directly in the face, pushing him right up against the back wall. Just as he thought he could not take it any longer, the forceful wind had gone, sucked into the vortex it had appeared from.

The man collected himself together, barely having any strength left to stand. "Is it over?" To him, his voice sounded wheezy.

"Come and see for yourself."

His stumbled his way across the clearing, peering over the edge with apprehension. The man was utterly speechless at the sight in front of him. The Sorceress's skeletal hands were scratching at the air, her bony fingers making slow and subtle movements. Her eyeless sockets stared at him blankly and her body restlessly shifted from side to side. She was alive and breathing and for that, he was grateful for the witches' intervention.

Yet, there was a part that nagged at him. Over the years, he had learnt to temper his expectations to more manageable levels. Before, he had always been a dreamer. His parents had once said it about him. His wife had said it. Even his friends had said it. But even so, as the man gaped at the Sorceress's decayed form, he couldn't help but question what the witches had actually achieved by performing the rune on her.

"She is alive," the first witch told him squarely, sensing his frustration.

"Barely," he shot back, rubbing his eyes just so he could make sure they weren't playing tricks on him. "I thought she might be, well..."

"Foolish Rufus Salt! You have a lot to learn about the revival incantation. She has been dead for a quarter of a century, not just a moon's turn! This Sorceress is alive, but remains extremely weak."

How can I rule an empire with just a living breathing corpse at my side?

"She will need the lifeblood of her own if she is to survive and prosper."

The lifeblood of her own...

Of course! Suddenly, the man had an incredible idea, one which he could not believe he hadn't thought of before. "I know where to find it. I..."

The witches had disappeared in a fit of cackles, as if they had never been there, leaving him alone with the Sorceress. Between his ears, he heard the witches miniscule voices speak out to him.

"We have paid our side of the bargain, Rufus Salt. And now you will be tied to our existence forever more."

"Forever more..." the second added.

"Forever more..." the third finished off.

He knew that their shrill tones and incessant cackling would be lodged inside his brain for eternity, but strangely, he had already accepted that. It was a small price to pay for what they had brought back to him. For what they had brought back to Focea.

"My lady," he spoke, reaching behind her neck and bringing her head to his chest in a deathly embrace. He could feel the Sorceress's jaw click open and shut. Open and shut. She was feeling her way into the world once more. Her skeletal hand then touched his paper thin forehead, stroking where a thick mop of hair had once been. A cry of exultation broke from him as she started to feel every single feature of his face.

"Soon, your skin will grow back and you will become more beautiful than ever before. Your power will grow beyond comprehension. This is only the beginning, my lady. This is only the beginning."

Two

The ship rocked from side to side as it rode across the waves, hurtling rapidly towards its destination. It had been a rocky ride from the outset, but calmer waters were now on the horizon, much to the relief of the ship's crew.

In the wooden cabin, excited chatter amongst the mercenaries onboard had now been replaced by silence as the enormity of the mission had now been realised. Four of the five Northwood Military Academy mercenaries onboard hadn't fought in a real life conflict before, including the elf who sat near the window. Opening his eyes, he looked across at his fellow passengers. The muscular young human to his left leant back with his hands behind his head, eyes shut tight. The elf had seen him around the academy several times before, but for the life of him couldn't remember his name. He then cast his gaze across to the male directly opposite, who had his head cupped in his hands. He looked as pale as a freshly washed sheet.

"Are you sure you're going to be ok, Finn?" the elf asked. He had been concerned for his roommate's welfare ever since the ship had departed from Northwood town harbour earlier in the day.

At first, Finn didn't reply, only staring at his comrade blankly. He gave his head a little shake to clear away the fuzziness and stood up shakily.

"Never better, Leonhard," he replied dryly to the elf, a hint of sarcasm present in his voice.

Finn had been boasting in the common room last night over a game of backgammon of how confident he felt in his first mission as a qualified mercenary. However, now the mission had arrived, Finn had looked increasingly worse for wear as the day wore on. Excusing himself, he ran towards the direction of the bathroom.

'*Gods, that must be at least ten times he's been in there now,*' Leonhard realised. It was true that Leonhard was just as nervous about the mission as his best friend, but he had a better way of hiding his emotions.

To make matters worse, the mercenaries hadn't been informed of what the mission involved or where they were going.

"The situation is changing all the time," General Francis Martine had said to the group before they had set sail. "You will be briefed on board as near to the mission start as possible."

Rumour had been rife at the academy this morning that they were heading into a combat zone somewhere to the west of Northwood island. Various locations had been mentioned, but having never set foot in the western part of the Terra continent, Leonhard didn't recognise any of them. He reached to his left and checked his bow and quiver of arrows, just to make sure he was prepared.

'*Still the same forty arrows I set sail with. But how many will I have left at the mission's end?*'

The chrome oil lamp above his head swayed lightly, replicating the movement of the ship. The cotton wick that burned inside the long glass chimney flickered, threatening to cast the cabin into relative darkness. It was clear to see that the steam powered academy vessel was from a bygone age, as it hadn't yet been equipped with electricity.

Leonhard was so preoccupied in his thoughts that he didn't see the woman enter the cabin.

"Finn doesn't look well," she said briskly, startling him somewhat.

Looking up, Leonhard realised it was the young woman known as Ella. He had learnt her name from Finn. She wore the traditional navy and studded silver academy uniform like the rest, but whilst the men's jackets had long sleeves, hers ended just above the shoulders. Ella also wore a yellow brooch above her left pocket as a tribute to her father, the Mayor of Northwood town. She had plaited her shiny brown hair at the back and her cheeks were flushed with nervous excitement.

Taking in her beauty, Leonhard immediately felt his face blush and turned his gaze towards the floor.

"Aw, he'll be fine once the mission starts," he replied in a hushed tone. He felt tense and his throat began to dry up. From the first time he had caught sight of Ella, Leonhard knew that he fancied her.

Ella stared back at the elf for a moment. She had noticed him from afar, but she had first gotten close to him as they sat down for their written examination three weeks ago. He had walked by her aisle and clumsily dropped his fountain pen at her feet. Quickly cursing himself for his error, he bent down to retrieve it. It was on his way up that their eyes met.

The elf intrigued Ella, having never encountered one before in her life. In fact, Leonhard was the only non-human currently at the academy. She felt compelled to discover why.

The elf was already at least a foot and a half taller than her despite being the same age and she knew that he would continue to grow further past his sixteen years. She thought it was amusing how he had started to grow blonde fuzz around his chin as a way to make himself look older than he actually was. However, it was his piercing blue eyes that she loved the most. She felt her heart flutter in her chest as he smiled at her, albeit briefly.

"Finn has always been a good talker," Ella said, with a brief chuckle. "Yet, saying and doing are two different things. Wait until he finds out who is our mission leader."

Leonhard looked up, puzzled. "General Martine, surely?"

"Sorry to disappoint you," Ella said. "It's Salamander."

Leonhard felt his heart sink instantly. Salamander Rourke was four years Leonhard's senior and had been at Northwood academy for some time. The man walked around like he owned the place and regularly picked on recruits he deemed weaker or inferior to himself. Leonhard had no idea that Salamander had even climbed on board the ship.

He turned his head and looked out of the small cabin window. General Martine was standing alone on deck, looking out to sea underneath a brilliant tangerine sky. He had mentioned to Leonhard before boarding that he wanted a word with him before the mission started. Now was his chance. Opening the door, Leonhard was instantly hit by a cold refreshing breeze, with the sharp taste of salt on his lips. The relief was palpable as the cabin had become hot and stifling. The highly polished wooden decking gleamed in the early evening light.

General Martine cocked his head at the approaching footsteps. He wore his trademark dark brown top hat, frayed around the edges from years of use. His matching marble cane was leaning against the gold painted banister. "How are you, Leonhard?" he asked, flicking ash away from a cigarette.

"I'm fine sir," Leonhard said. "A little nervous, though."

Martine nodded his head. "Nerves are good, as long you don't let them take over. The mission could be testing, but I'm confident you will all get through it."

Leonhard brushed his shoulder length blonde hair away from his face. "Ella tells me that Salamander is leading the mission, sir," he said. He secretly crossed his fingers that she was telling a lie.

Martine smiled briefly. "I see you're not pleased by that," he said. "I know you two haven't exactly seen eye to eye in the past. But he is a fine soldier and he wanted to lead a mission before he leaves Northwood."

Leonhard knew the institution held a tutorship programme where students who had qualified would support undergraduates for two years before they moved on to what Martine hoped would be a future military career. Some even went on to teach at Northwood, although Leonhard was relieved to hear that Salamander wasn't.

"Besides, he jumped at the chance to lead it," the General said. He said it with a finality that suggested the matter was closed.

"Sir, what did you want to talk to me about?" Leonhard asked, a little frustrated. It clearly wasn't Salamander's leadership qualities.

Throwing his cigarette overboard, Martine immediately lit a fresh one, blowing smoke high into the air as he puffed out.

"I know this isn't the best time to tell you this before the mission. But, you do need to know." He placed a firm hand on Leonhard's shoulder. "It's about your father. I must speak bluntly. He has disappeared!"

Leonhard staggered backwards from the rail in disbelief. He stared back blankly at the General, unable to speak.

"We are still unsure of the details at the moment," General Martine continued. "We do know that he left your home in a hurry." He softened his gaze at Leonhard. "Did he say anything to you last time you saw him?"

It had been six months since Leonhard had last seen his father. As the academy had broken up for an extended holiday, he had travelled back to his childhood home in the Elvish city of Ilsthyr on the heavily forested eastern side of the continent. It was the weekend of the Moonlight festival, an annual event where the Elf King would choose a new High Priest. At King Luthai's side stood Leonhard's father, performing his duty as the Royal

Bodyguard. Ruven Solveig was one of the King's most trusted aides and he hadn't given any indication to Leonhard then that anything was amiss. *'Why would he have left?'* Leonhard thought. To his mind, it just didn't make sense.

"He said nothing to me, sir," he replied simply. It was all he could say.

Martine looked at him with a sad smile. "You would tell me if he did, wouldn't you?" he asked, narrowing his gaze.

'Is the General accusing me of lying?'

The way Martine pressed for an answer made Leonhard feel slightly uncomfortable. Suddenly, a grizzly voice shouted from above, breaking the sudden tension.

"Apologies, sir," the captain of the ship spoke. The man, simply known to everyone at Northwood as Hobbs, was a small bald fellow with brown stubs for teeth. The vessel's two large funnels above him expelled steam high into the air. "We are nearing the destination, General."

Martine took off his top hat and brushed back his thinning hair, acknowledging Hobbs that he had heard him.

"It's time for me to brief you all on the mission," he said to Leonhard. "I will meet you downstairs."

Martine had started to walk away and then paused a moment.

"I need you to put this out of your mind for now and concentrate on the mission," he said with an authoritative tone. "We will talk more once it is over. Agreed?"

Leonhard had no choice but to nod his head. He scanned the horizon ahead, lost in his thoughts. For the first time since leaving Northwood, there was something else to see other than the endless ocean. In the far distance, a port town sat at the edge of a mountainous basin. He had expected to be venturing into a battlefield, with fire and smoke rising high into the air. Instead, it all seemed relatively calm.

'How odd. Maybe the battle is further inland, if indeed we are going into battle.'

Leonhard knew the prospect of his first mission should excite him, but his father's disappearance had now overshadowed the whole thing. He thought back again to any clues that his father may have given him that something was wrong, but Leonhard had nothing to go on. Certainly, his father's personality had changed somewhat since the death of Leonhard's mother ten years ago in childbirth. The man had retreated into himself a little and had become more reserved, particularly in his relationship with his son. However, he still served the King as faithfully as he ever did and to pack up and leave without saying a word was totally out of character.

And more importantly, why was Martine telling him this now? Could it not have waited until the mission had finished? It was clear he would have to wait to get back to Northwood to find out any more answers. Aware that the General would be waiting for him downstairs, Leonhard brushed his windswept hair from his face and went back into the cabin to retrieve his weapon.

With his head bent over the white ceramic sink, Finn splashed his face and rinsed his mouth out to get rid of the taste of vomit. He looked back at his reflection in the circular mirror with dread. His eyes were bloodshot and glassy. His curly black hair stood up in tufts at the side, almost giving the impression of two horns.

'I look like death warmed up,' the young man reflected bitterly.

It was true that Finn had never been a good sea traveller, but he knew that pre-mission nerves were more of a contributing factor towards his current predicament.

'That, and the fact I drank more than I should have done last night.'

Ignoring repeated warnings from Leonhard and his other roommates, Finn carried on playing cards and drinking spirits until the small hours. By the time he got to bed, the room was spinning and dawn had begun to break on the horizon.

'Never again,' he promised himself, not for the first time.

A sense of guilt also trickled through him. Finn had had a secret admiration for General Martine ever since he joined the academy two years ago and he didn't want to let him down, especially today of all days.

He remembered vividly his first visit to Northwood Academy. Worried by his increasing hyperactivity and falling grades in school, Finn's mother had arranged a meeting with the General to see if her son could join the academy instead. Finn remembered walking around open-mouthed in wonderment, amazed at the size of the place and by how regimented the students seemed. The General clearly saw something in the teenager and enlisted him immediately.

"I remember what I was like at school," Martine had said to Finn on his first day, sitting with him in his office. "I never felt sustained and I didn't want to be confined to the limitations of education."

The General then held his hands high up into the air, reminding Finn of something that a religious leader would do when preaching a sermon to his followers. "That is why I founded this academy."

'He would be disappointed if he saw me now,' Finn thought, shaking away the memory.

The clicking of the latch on the bathroom door made him jump. He wiped the steam from the mirror with his hand and saw Salamander enter the confined room. The man whistled a small tune as he relieved himself at the urinal and walked over to the basin next to Finn.

"Not feeling well, Finley?" Salamander asked. A small smirk worked its way across his broad face as he washed his hands and began combing his flaming red hair with a wide toothed comb.

Hearing his full name made Finn shudder. Only his mother called him Finley when she was cross with him, which in truth was often. Still, it was better than Salamander making reference to his large ears, spotty complexion or his big black glasses.

"I'll be fine," he snapped back.

"Good," Salamander said. "It's quite a team I've been lumbered with isn't it? An elf, a woman...and you. Thank God that the other mercenary is competent."

Finn brushed off the criticism. "So it's your team is it?" he asked. Finn had feared the worst when he saw Salamander waiting at Northwood docks.

"That's right, I am your leader. So, you do what I say! Understood?"

Ignoring him, Finn turned towards the door. Salamander's hand reached across and grabbed the well-worn gold handle, blocking Finn's exit.

"I was asking you a question," Salamander said, raising his voice.

A wild thought entered Finn's head. He would have loved nothing more than to grab Salamander's hand and twist it until he cried out for mercy. Again though, he knew how disappointed General Martine would be with him. Besides, Salamander was older and much stronger than Finn, so probably would have beaten him to a pulp.

"Aye, I heard ya," Finn said. "You say jump, I ask how high."

Salamander didn't look amused by Finn's joke. "I'm serious."

Finn didn't have any time for the man's macho mood. "Yeah? Well, I am too," he said, his face darkening. "Now are you gonna let me out or what?"

Salamander reluctantly released his grip from the handle. "General Martine is downstairs waiting to start the mission brief. It wouldn't do to keep him now, would it?"

Whilst Salamander followed Finn below deck, Ella had been watching Leonhard as he spoke to General Martine. She could tell by his stance that something was troubling him. His expression as he entered the cabin further reinforced Ella's concern.

"It's nothing," Leonhard had said when asked, speaking barely beyond a whisper.

She knew he was lying, but chose not to press it any further.

Downstairs, General Martine was busy reading a report given to him from Xai, the academy field operative. The woman had been present for each of the mercenaries practical examinations at the Northwood Mountain Temple, which overlooked the academy. Like the rest, she wore a navy blue uniform, with orange shoulder pads signifying she was a senior member of staff.

The briefing room was sparsely decorated, save for a large map of the world filling one wall and an inconspicuous oak table, which General Martine stood behind. As the students gathered around him, Leonhard caught a glance at Salamander. He replied with a sly wink. As much as he tried, Leonhard couldn't get rid of the thought that Salamander was up to no good.

"Alright everybody, settle down," the General began. "We are close to our destination, which is the town of Sleima on the Nulrassa coast." He pointed with his cane towards a small black dot on the east coast. "The town's militia captain, Geralde Basquet, contacted the academy twenty one hours ago for additional support. He told us that the town has come under attack."

"I wonder if the Foceans are behind it?" Ella whispered.

"Who?" Leonhard asked. He had barely heard Martine start his brief, as thoughts of Salamander clouded his head.

"The region of Nulrassa used to be part of the old Focean empire," she explained. "It broke away and declared independence after the empire's collapse. Maybe the Foceans are trying to invade and take it back."

With Leonhard still rather fresh in his integration into human society, Ella didn't blame the elf for not having heard of any of these places. She, on the other hand, had a deep knowledge of history, thanks to her stories from her father. Ella vividly remembered them both sitting in their observatory, fascinated by all of the stories of the famous leaders and important battles that the Mayor used to tell his daughter about. Her father had secretly wished for Ella to follow in his footsteps and become a politician. However, she knew from a young age that her skill with a sword was just as mighty as with words, so, much to her father's annoyance, she made the decision to leave home and join the academy.

"According to our latest reports, the majority of fighting has taken place in the hills surrounding Sleima castle, with the Nulrassan militia force thus far defending the town," Martine continued. "We will act as a second line of defence, in case the Foceans breaks through. Mayor Basquet has hired us for forty eight hours, with reinforcements from the academy at Godeburg too." The General paused for a moment, focusing solely on Leonhard.

"Salamander Rourke has been selected as the leader for this mission. He has been given set parameters on how to proceed. It goes without saying that you are all expected to follow his lead."

Leonhard noticed Xai looking nervous and uncomfortable. He wondered if she had similar reservations about the choice of mission leader. Just as Leonhard decided that he would have a quiet word with her, the ship's engine began to slow to a cruise. An unanticipated loud bang from underneath the ship sent the mercenaries to enter a momentary panic. The vibrations of the unknown impact caused Leonhard to stumble over towards the far wall, whilst General Martine's briefing papers went flying in all directions across the room. Confusion was emblazoned across Finn and Ella's face.

"Line up behind me!" Salamander barked at each of the four mercenaries. "We are about to land. Have your weapons at the ready!"

Leonhard decided it was now or never. Martine hadn't listened to him, but Xai just might be able to overturn the decision before it was too late. He raced over and grabbed her arm. She turned around and looked at him with a mixture of surprise and puzzlement.

"Leonhard, your captain is giving you an order," she said. "Go and line up!"

"It is about Salamander," he said. He was struggling to make himself heard over the ship's fans that had whirled into life. "I think he's up to something."

She shook her head and pointed to her ears. She hadn't heard him.

"Something isn't right!," he shouted in her ear. "We need to abort the mission!" He knew it sounded ridiculous as soon as it left his lips.

It was the sudden change in Xai's temperament that caused Leonhard's blood to run cold. There was fury in those eyes, but something hidden underneath too. Was it panic? Or fear?

"Get in line!" she ordered him, her face turning a beetroot red.

With his pleas falling on deaf ears, Leonhard began to trudge over to the doorway as the ship made contact with the soft sand of the beach. The vibration inside the ship again caused Leonhard to lose his footing. Mercifully, he managed to grab hold of the banister just in time.

"I must admit it mate, I have a bad feeling 'about this," Finn said, suddenly looking a lot younger than his sixteen years.

'Me too, Finn,' Leonhard thought to himself. He looked towards Salamander, who flashed him a hideous, twisted grin on the stairs. A cold chill crept up Leonhard's spine, raising the hair on the back of his neck. He took his late mother's necklace out of his pocket and kissed it once for luck. *'Me too!'*

Three

Stepping off the ship onto the empty beach, the five mercenaries noticed that dusk had fallen over Sleima. It was a clear evening, with a shadow of the silver moon overhead. There was a slight chill in the air, making Leonhard shudder as he proceeded along the beach.

"We have been hired for forty eight hours," General Martine had reminded them. "If not before, I will see you all here at dusk in two days' time. I wish you all luck."

The General had provided them with a satchel each which contained enough water and food to last them for the mission duration, as well as a homemade first aid kit.

First aid had been part of the curriculum at Northwood; Leonhard had coped moderately well in the classroom, but now he was in the field for real, his mind became a blur. He took a quick look inside the green box, surveying its contents and placed it back in his satchel. He prayed he wouldn't have to use first aid for the mission ahead.

Salamander pointed to a small copse of trees at the far side of the beach. "We will head through the woods and follow the path into town," he said, speaking with a commanding voice. "It's a town I know well. Do what I say and have your wits about you!"

Leonhard glanced back towards the vessel. With Xai having returned below deck, General Martine looked a lonely figure. He sensed Leonhard's gaze and tipped his hat in acknowledgement.

'You will be fine,' his look seemed to suggest. Leonhard returned a nervous smile and caught up with the other mercenaries, passing the splintered wreck of a wooden fishing boat that protruded from the sands.

"I don't believe it!" Finn said. "We've only jus' stepped off the goddamn ship and Salamander is already bossin' us around."

"Watch him close," Leonhard warned. "I don't trust him!"

"Me neither." Finn fished into his jacket pocket and pulled out a black and gold speckled bandana, which he duly tied around his forehead.

"What in God's name is that?

"It's my good luck charm," Finn said, grinning.

Leonhard couldn't remember him ever wearing it before, even during their downtime. "Has it ever given you luck then, Finn?"

"Nope," he replied, shaking his head. "But there's always a first time, ain't there?"

As Salamander stood impatiently up the beach, Finn introduced Leonhard to Percy, the other mercenary in the group. The lad was only a couple of inches shorter than Leonhard and shook the elf's hand with an easy grip. "I've seen you in the practise yard," he said, acknowledging the quiver of arrows on Leonhard's back. "You're really good with your aiming."

The praise from Percy brought a blush to his cheeks. Leonhard actually hadn't received much in the way of encouragement since his mother had died. He could only offer a hushed thanks in response.

"Yeah, Percy is the captain of the academy Hardball team," Finn said, almost in a mocking way. "Maybe you should think about joinin', Leonhard."

In truth, Leonhard could think of nothing worse. The sport of Hardball, an extremely popular human sport, was renowned for its rough and physical nature. Leonhard's slender physique would be seemingly at odds with the makeup of a traditional Hardball player. He had seen Finn enter the trials for the team once and fail miserably. Heaven knows why Finn thought Leonhard would fare any better.

Salamander walked over cockily, chuckling to himself.

"Are you serious, Finley? An elf playing hardball? That'll be the day!"

Ella side-stepped Leonhard hastily and came face to face with Salamander. "You're a fine one to talk, aren't you?" she said, jabbing her middle finger towards his wide chest. "I can't recall ever hearing that you made it onto the team."

Ella's challenge only served to amuse Salamander. "And I cannot 'recall' asking for a woman's opinion on the subject." He cocked his head upwards. "Leonhard's a big boy. He can defend himself, right?"

Ella felt the anger rise up inside her. She was in two minds whether to instigate the argument further. The man infuriated her immensely. However, she knew this was her first proper mission and she had to keep professional. Reluctantly, she stood down, whispering the words "sexist pig" under her breath.

Out of nowhere, Salamander placed his hand over the leather hilt of his short sword.

"Say that again woman, I dare you," he cried, baring his teeth in a snarl.

The other three mercenaries stood around her, speechless. Leonhard couldn't believe their mission leader was prepared to use his weapon against his own team. He again looked at the beached vessel. General Martine had followed Xai below deck.

'If only you were watching your precious mission leader now, you would see him for what he really was,' he thought bitterly.

"That's enough, Salamander!" he then shouted with an authoritative voice that shocked even himself. "If you don't calm yourself down and lead the mission, I am going straight back to the ship and will force the General to appoint a new leader. Understood?" Feeling the blood pounding in his ears, he worked his shoulders to relieve the tension.

Salamander knew Leonhard had him cornered. He couldn't care less what Martine thought about him, but in order for his 'secret plan' to succeed, he needed to be the one who led the mission.

"Fine," Salamander said, with a look of hatred in his eyes. "She's not worth it anyway."

As the mercenaries followed him towards the wood, Salamander smiled to himself. He knew his chance for revenge would come soon enough.

The mission leader slowed the pace down underneath the gnarled branches, seemingly worried that the crunch of leaves underfoot would give their position away to the enemy. There was no sign yet of any battle reaching the beach, but Leonhard did wonder if the Focean army had received word of reinforcements arriving and had posted spies in the woods to take them out before they could reach the town proper. Certainly, the lack of light between the trees would put them at a disadvantage if they were attacked.

Approaching a fork in the pathway, the recruits followed the dirt path to the left hand side, passing an abandoned stone hut. Moss had completely covered two sides of the walls, with the roof badly damaged by years of neglect. Ella thought she heard a noise rustling in the undergrowth behind the building and went around the back to investigate. She was slightly embarrassed to find only a grey squirrel hunting for acorns amongst the fungi. It spied her sword and clambered up the nearest tree.

Glancing at the ruined building, Leonhard felt his breath caught in his throat. His blood turned to ice and the hairs on the back of his neck stood on end. He drew his jacket closer over his body, wondering if the others felt the same as he did. The shadows began to darken around the building, highlighting the white-wash stone. For some inexplicable reason, Leonhard could feel the presence of evil radiating from the tumbledown walls.

'This is stupid!' he realised. 'The place is clearly empty.' Still, a strange presence drew him to it.

"You alright, mate?" Finn asked, placing a hand on his shoulder.

The darkness obliterated itself in an instant, as if someone had turned on a light.

"I don't know," Leonhard replied in a hushed voice. "Did you not feel it?"

"I feel hungry and a little nervous, if that's what you mean."

This was no time for jokes. Leonhard couldn't explain to Finn what he had felt, but he had an urge to move away from the hut as soon as possible. He took one curious look at the building and followed the others through the woods.

The twisting path eventually led them towards the town's docks. A flock of squawking seagulls took off towards the shimmering sea as they heard the approaching group. The seabirds had been helping themselves to some food that a litterbug had casually left.

"Bloody things," Salamander said, kicking a plastic carton over the side of the walkway into the water below. Waves splashed meekly back and forth against the concrete pier, with only a handful of vessels moored in the docks. Further along the boardwalk were grimy wooden shacks that housed the town's poorer citizens, nestled up against the high town walls. Parts of the maze of wooden walkways between the buildings had broken away, with painted graffiti everywhere. Rubbish had been piled high in the centre of the slum, drawing the attention of several thousand flies. The majority of the hovels looked empty, with its residents presumably enlisting in the war effort. Looking at the way Sleima had treated its destitute, Leonhard found it rather contradicting that its leader had called on the poor to serve in their hour of need.

Doubling back on themselves, the mercenaries crossed a stone white bridge, passing underneath the ancient town walls. The difference in wealth became immediately apparent inside the town proper; rich apartment buildings with ornate balconies had been built alongside expensive looking hotels. As was the case at the dockside, the town appeared eerily quiet, with the majority of the buildings having had their shutters drawn across. Sleima's ancient castle loomed large above the town, with its round towers illuminated in vivid orange lighting.

"According to Martine, the Foceans ventured through the mountain range at the back of the castle," Salamander said. He took a toothpick out of his jacket pocket and placed it in his mouth in an effort to make himself look cooler. "If Basquet were to make a stand, that's where it would be."

"Well, I can't hear any fightin'," Finn said, looking unperturbed.

"I agree," Salamander said, to the surprise of the others. He pointed at the main street that worked its way up a sharp incline. "Let's keep moving."

As they ventured further upwards into the town, the smell of smoke lingered in the air. Mist from the sea rose up the hill, enveloping the town in a sinister shroud. Hexagonal street lights illuminated the twisty cobbled streets in a strange white light.

Leonhard held himself back, waiting for Ella to catch up with him. He felt his pulse quicken, but he tried to ignore the nerves the best he could. He felt compelled to speak to her about the incident with Salamander on the beach.

"I'm sorry for what happened back there," he said to her, being careful to keep his voice down. "You shouldn't have to put up with any of that."

Ella's smile was dry, but her eyes twinkled in gratitude.

"That Salamander really winds me up. What was the General thinking in appointing him as mission leader?"

"I really don't know," Leonhard said. It was a good question, one which he didn't have an answer to. Salamander had always been hot headed, quick to react without thought or reason.

The first time Leonhard had seen him in person was in the academy practise yard, in the midst of a duel with a student called Timothee. At first, the fight was pretty even, both striking and blocking blows with efficient ease. Yet, with both fearing a loss in front of an ever increasing crowd, the fight had turned nasty. Salamander ended the fight by kicking his opponent in the chest and striking his short sword at Timothee's face. The student had stayed in the infirmary for over a month afterwards, leaving the academy with a large twisted scar stretching from his forehead to his left cheek. Like many, Leonhard had been flabbergasted to hear that Salamander had only received a reprimand for his actions.

"I can't believe he was actually going to raise his sword at me," Ella said. Even in the low level light, Leonhard could see her cheeks were covered with tears.

He suddenly felt uneasy, unsure how to react. Leonhard had never been confident in speaking to girls, despite having modest attention from them back home. He contemplated putting his arm around Ella to comfort her. *'No, no!'* he thought. *'That's way too forward!'*

He decided to speak some comforting words instead, aiming to cheer her up.

"I, I mean we, will...er...keep you safe from him. Don't worry!" He smiled, pleased at his good natured kindness.

Yet, it was quickly evident from Ella's reaction that it was the worst thing Leonhard could have said. Her nostrils flared and her lips pursed shut.

"I don't need you to protect me!" she cried out, causing the others to turn towards the source of the commotion. "I am more than capable of protecting myself, thank you very much!" She stormed off up the street, leaving Leonhard stunned at her reaction.

'What did I say? I really do not understand women!'

He looked up towards a misshapen black and white beamed apartment. The upper floor protruded away from the rest of the building and overlooked the main street. From the central window, an elderly woman gazed down at him with suspicion, turning her craggy face into a sneer. Leonhard felt like sticking a finger up at her in his frustration, but instead, he kicked the nearest lamp post with his foot and carried on in a huff.

Salamander led the group straight on at a junction and up a steep hill towards a tall glass faced clocktower. The hands on the clock face showed the group the time of half past two; it had clearly stopped working.

Finn could feel the muscles in his legs already begin to ache from all the walking. To make matters worse, the cobblestones were slick from rain earlier that day. He had almost lost his footing a couple of times, but to his relief, the rest of the group were also struggling up the hill. As he explored the town further, he noticed one obvious difference to his hometown of Northwood; there were no road vehicles here at all. It was true that the limited space would have made it hard for cars to pass each other, but compared to the heavy traffic that plagued his hometown, Finn found it very odd.

Now that his stomach had settled down, he caught a quick breather. He fished into his canvas rucksack and helped himself to a piece of cake from the rations. He was extremely pleased to find it was a large Northwood tart, which was his favourite sweet.

'You know me well, General,' Finn thought, devouring the cake rapidly. Leonhard charged past him with his head down, muttering something inaudible. He called out his friend to see what the problem was but received no answer.

Finn had been friends with Leonhard for two years, yet he still felt as if he didn't properly know the elf. He found him to be an enigma. They were polar opposites in personality; whilst Finn was brash, loud and untidy, Leonhard was a shy, reserved and extremely organised person. Sharing a room with a non-human had been strange at first, but Finn had gotten used to Leonhard's habits pretty quickly. He knew when to give his friend space. Leonhard would pray every night to his elf gods and was often deep in contemplation. His facial expression at this moment in time suggested that he was having one of those moments.

Finn had suspected Leonhard fancied Ella ever since he had asked him for her name. It was the first time he ever mentioned anything about a girl to him, so to Finn, she must have made an impression on him.

And to be fair, Ella was a fine looking woman. Finn had been in the same school as her when he was younger, so they knew each other fairly well. He had actually fancied her at one point, but quickly knew he was in a different league to the boys she was actually interested in.

A deep cry from Percy alerted him back to the mission at hand.

"Someone's there!" the mercenary shouted, pointing to an approaching figure in the street. The shadow stumbled towards them slowly through the mist, bouncing off a nearby wall.

The person is either wounded from the battle or blind drunk,' Finn realised. As the figure moved closer, he quickly realised it was both. It was a young soldier with a dirty, brown beard. He wore a bronze coloured leather jerkin that certainly wouldn't offer much protection in battle. The grimace on his face and the way he clutched his stomach suggested the soldier was in serious pain. As the street lights lit his features further, Finn could see that the majority of his front was covered in a dark red stain that could only be blood.

The aromas of dirt and sweat filled his nose, making him gag. He immediately realised there was another odour underneath the surface also; the sweet, stale smell of alcohol. It was obvious that the man had been drinking before the battle.

"Are you the enemy?" the soldier asked heavily, speaking with a thick foreign accent. He held a finger under Leonhard's chin and studied the elf with mild puzzlement.

"It depends who you're fighting for," Salamander said.

"Why Nulrassa, of course! At least I was. It's a rout up there! The Foceans had us surrounded." The soldier paused to cough up a globule of phlegm. "They were using weapons from the depths of hell!"

'Weapons from hell?' Finn wondered. *'The man must be crazy!'*

"Aye, they had reinforcements too." The soldier regarded them each with a suspicious eye. "In fact they were all young ones like yourselves."

General Martine had announced that there would be students from another academy assisting the mission. Finn hadn't heard of the Godeburg academy before, but in his mind, he expected a similar sort of setup to

Northwood. He was fairly surprised not to see another vessel parked up on the beach.

'If the man is telling the truth, why is Godeburg fighting for Focea when we are fighting for Nulrassa?' It just didn't make sense.

"Enough!" Salamander cut in. "Leave us and crawl back to the hole that you came from!"

"How dare you!" the soldier said, slurring his words. "I will not stand here whilst enemy soldiers walk my streets." He took his hand away from his bleeding wound and slowly unsheathed his rust covered katana sword.

Before Leonhard could make a desperate plea for the soldier to leave and tend to his wounds, Salamander held his weapon out, ready to fight. The pair clashed swords twice before Salamander drove his short sword through the soldier's chest, sending him immediately to the ground. To rub salt in the wounds, Salamander wiped his weapon clean on the man's sleeve. "That's how you kill a man," he said to them, boasting. He began to walk away with a cocky stride.

The four new recruits stood shell-shocked by their leader's actions. Finn found that he couldn't take his eyes off the crimson red blood gushing from the soldier's chest. It was only Leonhard that had seen someone die before; his father had invited him to a jousting festival when he was ten to celebrate King Luthai's thirtieth year on the throne. To this day, Leonhard remembered vividly the point of the spear splintering and impaling the challenger in the neck.

"Are you just going to stand there and watch him die?" Salamander called back to them, encouraging them to continue. "There will be plenty more like him ahead."

Red faced, Ella blazed with anger.

"Does it not bother you that you've just ended a life?" she cried, pacing across the street to him at a relentless speed. "He could have had a wife and children, you know. You've just taken that away!"

"It makes no odds to me who he was," Salamander replied, shrugging his shoulders. "He challenged me and I accepted. We are in a battlefield sweetheart, unless you have forgotten."

Hearing the word 'sweetheart' made Ella's skin crawl.

"You know something! You're so…" She paused, trying to think of one word that would sum up Salamander perfectly.

"I'm what, woman? Spit it out, I'm dying to know!"

"Condescending! That's what you are!"

"Ha! Such a big word for a little lady."

An abrupt series of large bangs came from the direction of the castle, ending Salamander and Ella's argument before it could flare up any further. The brutal sounds of battle filled the air, as screaming intertwined itself with loud cheering. The castle became surrounded by smoke and fire, but the building had seemingly remained untouched. The fight had seemingly reached Sleima.

At the top of the street, Salamander positioned the group next to a marble fountain in the centre of the town square. The buildings surrounding the square seemed still and lifeless. Above them, the castle looked as imposing as any building Leonhard had ever seen. Even from this distance, he could decipher the spikes that lined the barricades, which allowed soldiers to walk between the castle's four round turrets. A gravel pathway zigzagged its way from the square to the castle entrance, with several dark shapes laying lifeless across the path. Leonhard gulped, realising they could only be soldiers, either dying or dead already.

'We have come too late for the Nulrassan militia,' he realised, shaking his head.

Percy let out a long sigh of frustration. "Now what do we do?" he asked. His loud tone echoed around the empty square.

"Keep your voice down will you?" Salamander said, scalding Percy with an angry look. "You all heard Martine's brief. This is as good as a place to wait as any."

Salamander actually spoke the truth. If the rebel force was to attack Sleima town, the only way they could reach it from the castle was to descend the grassy hill. Still, Leonhard was surprised as anybody to find Salamander following the General's orders. Usually, the man would rush headlong into battle. Again, the niggling feeling that he was up to something refused to disappear.

The moon was high in the night sky as the group waited for any sign of the enemy. Apart from the odd bang and shout, the battle seemed to have played itself out. Sitting beside the flowing fountain, Leonhard called across to Finn for the time.

"Eight o'clock," Finn replied, checking his watch. "We've only been here for an hour. It feels like a day already!"

Although he wouldn't freely admit it, this hadn't been exactly how Leonhard had imagined his first mission. His dreams over the last couple of nights had repeatedly consisted of his team surrounded by the enemy in a forest, with the battle seemingly lost. Unseen, Leonhard had climbed a nearby tree and began dispatching the soldiers one by one with his arrows. Descending to rapturous applause, he received a heroic kiss from Ella on the lips. It was a magical way to end a dream.

The reality of the mission so far had shattered that illusion completely. Being here seemed like a complete waste of time. Furthermore, every time he looked towards Ella's direction, she scowled and turned her head away. She was evidently still mad at him.

Knowing something was troubling his friend, Finn pulled Leonhard to one side and asked him what was wrong.

"It's nothing," he said.

"Come on man, I know ya better than that. Ella told me that you spoke to the General on the ship. Was it bad news?"

"It was about my father, Finn." Leonhard turned, making sure Salamander wasn't overhearing. "He's disappeared!"

"Disappeared? Man, that's bad! Did he say anythin' else?"

Leonhard shook his head. "He only wants me to concentrate on the mission. I mean, how can I do that not knowing where my father is or what he's gotten himself into?"

Finn placed his hand on his shoulder. "If it's any easier, I know how ya feel."

Leonhard knew that when Finn had been a toddler, his father had gone out to sea to fish and had never returned. He thanked Finn all the same, but it still didn't make him feel better. In fact, thinking that his father might be lost forever in the same way as Finn's actually made him feel worse.

Percy, meanwhile, had grown restless, pacing constantly around the town square. He had started to swing his sword into thin air, eager for anything that would resemble a fight.

"Don't do that," Salamander said across to him.

"Why?" Percy growled.

"It's annoying. Besides, you look as if you're swatting flies."

"We're wasted here, Salamander! Surely you can see that?"

Salamander smiled. "Not exactly how you imagined your first mission, Percy? You'll find in your military career that some missions are tedious, whilst some get the adrenaline pumping. It's all the same to me."

"I fail to believe that," Ella said, breaking her stony silence.

"Believe what you want." Salamander stood up, stretching out his arms, yawning. "I'll tell you what, Percy. Me and the elf over there will keep watch here, whilst you and the others take a look around. How does that sound?"

Percy eagerly retrieved his satchel from the steps of the fountain, not needing to be asked twice.

"What if the Foceans make their way through?" he asked Salamander.

"I'll shout."

"We might not hear you."

"I'll shout loudly. Now go!"

Ella and Finn followed Percy down a side street to the left of the square. The cobbles were well worn in places and some had broken off entirely, making navigation in the low light tricky. As they passed a deserted cemetery, Finn became increasingly nervous. The silhouettes of the gravestones in the moonlight made eerie shapes against the trees. Feeling spooked, Finn diverted his attention away, glancing up at the castle that dominated the skyline. From the front, the building had looked in a relatively healthy state. However, he noticed that the walls on its left side had fallen away to ruins. In his wonderment, he failed to see two children run out into the road. Both of the children dropped their toy cars in surprise and stared at each of the mercenaries quizzically.

"Where's Daddy?" a snot nosed boy asked in a tatty collared shirt. Judging by his size, he was the youngest of the pair.

"Dunno, lad," Finn said. "He ain't with us."

Tutting at the lack of compassion from his colleague, Ella knelt down and put her hands on the boy's shoulders. He was clearly shaken from his father's absence, as well as the sounds from the nearby battle.

"Did your Dad go to fight in the battle?" she asked them, changing her voice to something more childlike.

The young boy stared back at her with wide eyes. Eventually, he nodded his head.

"I'm sure he will be back soon." She looked behind the two children and saw a portly woman standing in the doorway of the house opposite. A black and white chequered pinny was tied around her large waist and she held a cat tightly in her right arm. By the way the grey feline was squirming, it wanted nothing more than to be free of the woman's firm grip.

"It's not safe on the streets," Ella warned the children. "Look, your mother's waiting for you!"

"That's not our mum," the eldest boy cheekily replied. "That's Marcella, our neighbour. She's too fat to fight."

"Which one of you said that?" the woman called out, stepping onto the street. She looked even larger as she hobbled closer. "Get inside now, both of you!"

Heads down, the children obeyed their neighbour. The woman known as Marcella cast a nervous glance up and down the street and slammed the front door shut in the mercenaries faces.

"Why did you get their hopes up?" Percy asked Ella. "Their parents are probably dead already."

"You don't know that!" Ella said, casting a look of despair at both men. She stormed off down the street, alone.

Percy's group had only just disappeared from sight when Salamander stretched out his long arms and started to walk across the square to the base of the hill.

"Where are you going?" Leonhard called out after him.

"I thought we could go for a wander ourselves," Salamander replied, regarding Leonhard with a sly and significant look. "Shall we?"

Leonhard knew Salamander's intentions were too good to be true. "But the orders were…"

"I know what the orders were, goddammit! In case you have forgotten, I am the mission leader and you do what I say!" In his hot temper, Salamander kicked a stone across the square. It only just missed Leonhard's leg, skipping across the cobbles and landing at the base of the fountain with a smack. He then stared at the sky for a moment, as if he was waiting for a sign.

"Besides, do you not want to see what has happened up at the castle?"

Leonhard secretly did.

'It will be on Salamander's head if there is any comeback, not mine,' he realised.

Secretly, he reached into his leather quiver on his back and placed an arrow on the ground, pointing directly at the castle. He hoped Finn and Ella would work out what it meant in case of trouble.

Salamander led Leonhard up the twisting path in a deafening silence. Half way up, they encountered the first fallen soldier. Dressed in the same brown outfit as the earlier soldier, Salamander turned the body over and was surprised to find it was a woman. She had blows to her neck and chest, but Leonhard was under no doubt that it had been the nasty wound to her head that had finished her off. The elf knelt and closed her eyelids in respect.

"Are you going to do that to every dead body we find?" Salamander chuckled. "It'll be a long climb if you do."

Leonhard ignored him the best he could and carried on up the hill.

Before they reached the top, the pair had passed over twenty fallen soldiers. All but one were wearing the bronze of Nulrassa. Smoke drifted into their faces, causing Leonhard's eyes to water. He turned his head, taking in the view of the town and the sea beyond.

The twinkling street lights gave Leonhard the impression of hovering fireflies. It seemed so calm, almost serene; a complete contrast to the bloodbath that had occurred outside the castle.

Splintered stakes and rusty swords were littered in the dirt, with crows already feasting on the corpses. The smell of death was everywhere. Leonhard felt his stomach lurch forward repeatedly. Trying to avoid the sight of the massacre, he spotted a silver object sparkle in the moonlight. He dug his hands into the dirt, pulling out several small metallic balls. Oddly, they were still warm to the touch.

"Are these bullets?" he asked.

"Correct," Salamander said. "I'm surprised 'you' know what they are."

Leonhard did indeed know what they were. An avid collector of all weapons, King Luthai of Ilsthyr had several rifles adorned on his walls, next to hundreds of swords, axes and bows. Firearm technology was renowned for being unpredictable and there were only a handful of sharpshooters in the world that could use them in a safe and effective manner. Observing the wounds of the dead, Leonhard could see that the Foceans had used these weapons on a much wider scale that had ever been known before.

"What militia force uses guns?" He felt a shiver work its way down his spine.

"It's not a militia," Salamander said. He pointed towards the wooden drawbridge, which had started to lower. As the portcullis was raised, hundreds of soldiers dressed in the heaviest golden armour Leonhard had ever seen marched towards them regimentally. "The Foceans have built themselves an army!"

As the armoured soldiers surrounded the pair in a semicircle, Leonhard loaded his bow. He looked to see if Salamander had drawn his weapon too. Worryingly, he hadn't.

The soldiers dispersed to let a tall, thin man through. His strides were so long that he made the distance up in no time. The man wore a long black leather coat that swayed with his movements and, for some unknown reason, he had covered his head with a dark veil.

"You're late, Salamander!" the man said threateningly. "You know I hate it when people are not on time."

Salamander paid no heed to the man. "I thought you might have been somewhat preoccupied, Rufus," he said calmly. He placed his right hand against Leonhard's back and forced him face first into the dirt. "Allow me to present you a gift."

"But he's just a boy!" the man quickly spat through the mouth slit in the veil, his voice booming in Leonhard's ears. He reached forward and grabbed the cuff of Salamander's navy jacket, pulling at him in anger. "I said to you I wanted Ruven Solveig! Yet, you bring me a boy." He brought his masked face closer and whispered in Salamander's ear. "Do you take me for a fool?"

Salamander's face paled, with his cocky exuberance extinguished in a flash. "Let...let me explain!" he said, sounding as young as a child. "This isn't just any boy. I bring you the son of Ruven Solveig."

The man known as Rufus looked down at Leonhard again, harder this time. His hands were ghostly white and he had strange red marks on his fingers. "This puny rat? You lie, Salamander! I know Ruven and he looks nothing like him."

Indeed, Leonhard's physical characteristics resembled more of his late mother than his father. The bleach blonde hair, coral blue eyes and slender hips all were at odds with his father's gruff appearance. Of course, Leonhard was desperate to know what had happened to his father, but secretly wondered if he could yet talk his way out of the situation.

"I've never heard of this Ruven he talks of," Leonhard lied. It sounded strange as soon as it left his mouth. "My father died when I was young. I don't know what game Salamander is playing with you but I am not the person you were promised!"

Salamander twisted his face in a deep fury. "Don't listen to him, Rufus," he said, striking Leonhard hard across his face. The elf again fell to the ground, spitting out blood.

"I've heard enough!" Rufus exclaimed. He gestured with a finger to his army. "Throw them both in the dungeons."

Sweat poured from Salamander's forehead. He attempted to wriggle away from the soldiers tight grip, but failed miserably.

"But I'm telling the truth!" he said in a panicked tone. "We had an agreement!"

Rufus stared back at him blankly, cupping his hands together. "For your sake Salamander, I hope you are telling the truth. There is only one way to find out."

Four

Percy, Finn and Ella continued to make their way through Sleima's twisting streets. They found them devoid of life, save for a stray fox-red Labrador dog. The animal twitched its large ears as the group approached and darted down a pitch black back street, scavenging for any food that may have fallen from the rubbish bins. Always eager to break any silence, Finn had entered a lengthy conversation with Percy about whether the academy's Hardball team should enter the professional league.

"Well, you have seen us play, Finn," Percy said. "General Martine has submitted our application to the governing body. I think we are ready."

Finn quickly scoffed at the notion. "Aye, I've seen you play other academies and reserve squads. Comin' up against a team like the Reno Racers though will be somethin' else entirely." The Reno Racers were the nearest professional team to Northwood and Finn had supported them adoringly since he was a child.

Percy knew Finn was fishing for an argument, as he was still extremely bitter about not being picked following the academy try-outs. As the captain of the team himself, Percy knew Finn was quick, but he had been tackled off the ball far too often. He contemplated on picking him for next year if the young man gained a bit of muscle and toughened himself up.

Meanwhile, Ella had become increasingly restless. She had deliberately kept her distance from the pair, lost in thought. As she ventured deeper into the town, she had started to share Finn and Leonhard's reservations about Salamander's intentions.

'I was too hard on Leonhard,' she thought, stopping to take on some water. In her youth, her mother had frequently compared Ella's temperament to that of a disturbed hornet's nest, criticising her daughter for a lack of patience.

'It seems you were right about me, mother.'

Ella just hoped her attitude wouldn't put Leonhard off. She called to the two men in front to turn back towards the square.

"Good idea," Finn agreed, casting a hard look at Percy. "There ain't nobody else here anyway."

The twang of guilt morphed into a sucker punch in the stomach as they returned to find the square empty.

"I thought Salamander was staying here," Percy said. "Where would they have gone?"

"Ain't it obvious," Finn said, looking up towards the castle. "I knew that prick was up to somethin'!' He then flexed his hands and pointed an accusing finger at Percy. "If you hadn't been so eager to leave, we may have been able to stop him!"

"Argh, get over yourself, Finn! I don't seem to remember you offering any resistance to Salamander's orders."

Pacing the square in vexation, Finn turned his head slowly towards Percy, staring at him suspiciously. "You knew what he was goin' to do, didn't you? I bet you have both planned this out and..."

"Stop it, the both of you!" Ella shouted. Whilst the two mercenaries had been arguing with each other, she had spotted an object on the ground glistening in the moonlight. "Look, Leonhard has left us a sign," she said, showing them both the arrow.

"Well, what are we waitin' for?" Finn said, marching past them insolently. He had already unsheathed his daggers, ready to do battle. "Let's rescue him!"

Ella was aghast at Finn's stupidity. She had seen him do some foolish things in their school, but this just about topped them all.

"I hardly think us three will be able to take them all on. No, I say we go back to the ship and tell General Martine what has happened."

Receiving agreement from Percy, she started back towards the main street, where a thick, breathless voice stopped her in her tracks. The General came into view seconds later, resting on his cane.

"There's no need to do that, Ella," he said, straightening his hat. "That hill sure is steep. I'm not as fit as I used to be." He pulled out a cigarette from the top pocket of his double breasted brown jacket and lit it instantly, inhaling the smoke with satisfaction.

"Well, 'they' probably have something to do with it, sir," Ella said impatiently, pointing at the cigarettes in disgust. Her grandparents had both been heavy smokers and died from resulting diseases. Again, she thought she may have gone too far and looked at the General sheepishly.

Luckily, Martine saw the funny side of it and smiled weakly.

"You are right Ella. They will be the death of me, no doubt." He then looked at the three mercenaries straight in the face, with all of the humour evaporated. "Tell me what happened."

"We heard the battle taking place outside the castle," Ella said. "Salamander ordered the three of us to have a look around, whilst him and Leonhard would remain here."

"It was only when we returned, we found them gone," Percy added.

To say Martine looked disappointed was an understatement. His eyebrows were drawn together in a deep frown.

"Salamander's orders were indeed to remain at this exact spot," he said. "After hearing nothing from Godeburg, I thought I'd come overboard to assess the situation myself."

He then noticed the two daggers gripped tightly in Finn's palms and eyed him distastefully. "So you were to lead the charge were you? I am disappointed in you, Finn."

To hear those words from the General hurt Finn more than anything. He sheathed his weapons at once, mentally kicking himself for his foolhardiness. "I...I only meant to help get Leonhard back," he said. It was a weak argument to be sure, but it gave his reasoning some context.

If the General had heard him, he made no reaction. Instead, his eyes were fixed on the hill leading up to the castle. A large group of soldiers descended the pathway, gathered in an informal huddle.

"We are compromised here," Martine said, remaining calm. He stubbed out the cigarette with his foot and kicked it out of sight towards the base of the fountain. "Let's move out."

The mercenaries positioned themselves in a dark alleyway opposite the main street. The ever increasing mist worked in their favour, as it allowed them to stand relatively close without being seen. At a count, over thirty Focean soldiers walked by minutes later, laughing and joking with each other. Stripped of their golden armour, the men still wore white padded gambesons to keep off the evening chill. Sewn into the right corner was a badge displaying the black and white sun crest of Focea. They spoke with heavy, slurred voices that suggested their victory celebrations had already begun in earnest.

"...threw the elf in the castle dungeon," one said with a heavy voice.

"What about the other one?" another asked.

"Cap'n Rufus is reprimanding him now," the first said, drawing choruses of laughter. "I'm glad I'm not in his shoes."

"Who cares about him?" the second fired back. "Come on, we've been ordered to plunder and burn this god-damned town. I for one intend to follow the Captain's orders!"

The soldier's proclamation drew a chorus of approval, all chanting 'Focea! Focea!' as they went in search of the nearest bar.

"Captain Rufus?" Martine whispered with a puzzled tone. "Surely not..."

"Sir?" Ella asked. "What is it?"

Martine waved a dismissive hand at her. "It doesn't matter. What does matter is figuring a way to break Leonhard out."

As Finn heard the soldiers boast about his friend, he felt the anger quickly rise up. Again, he had to bite back the urge to run up the hill towards the castle entrance. "Do you have any ideas, sir?" he asked.

"Indeed. During my youth, I served in the Akiran militia. One particular expedition saw us stop here at Sleima, where we tended to our wounds and replenished our supplies. The Mayor at the time had a problem with a local group of bandits and asked us all to help him out." Martine held his tongue for a moment as more soldiers walked past in the same good mood as the others. "I won't bore you with the details, but we eventually caught them. One particular day, I was on guard duty in the castle dungeons and found a trapdoor at the far end. When it came to changing over, I followed it and discovered the tunnel led all the way to a series of caves underneath the castle." He pointed a long finger towards the vicinity of the docks. "If we steal a boat, we could row around the cliffs and break in that way."

Nodding their heads in agreement, the group stealthily made their way through the back streets of Sleima, heading downwards towards the docks. Martine guided the young mercenaries as well as he could remember, keeping as close to the well-lit main street as he dared to. As he approached each intersection, he would hold his hand up to halt the group, whilst he took a moment to glance around the corner.

The alleyways were incredibly dark, with only the moonlight to guide them in places. On one occasion, Finn walked straight into an unsighted washing line and went flying. He upended the pole the wire had been attached to, sending it and the damp clothes clattering to the floor. The noise seemed to echo around them for over a minute. To Finn's relief though, no one else had heard the commotion.

The group could hear the loud crackling of fire and the sharp taste of smoke even before they passed back underneath the town walls. A large group of Foceans had begun burning the dockyard slums to the ground. The wooden structures burned immediately, sending plumes of hot orange light into the air.

"I remember there used to be a good tavern in there," Martine whispered, looking longingly at the slums. "Sure, you had to watch who you spoke to, but the ale cost a fraction of what it did in town."

The General scouted the wharf and found a suitable rowing boat that would fit the four of them in. The soldiers were too busy to see them sneak past, seemingly mesmerised by the roaring fire. He then got to work untying the heavily knotted rope from the mooring post and handed a chipped oar to Finn.

"This moonlight will make it easier for them to spot us, so we must keep close to the shadow of the pier," he instructed. "Row slowly and don't make a sound!"

Finn hadn't picked up an oar before in his life. His mother had always told him to stay away from the docks in Northwood, seemingly afraid that Finn would be swept away out to sea and lost like his father.

'That was then and this is now,' he told himself, plucking up some courage. He knew this was the only plausible way to break into the castle. Also, he was eager to make amends with the General, so he took the oar from him at once.

Martine ordered Ella and Percy to keep a look out for the enemy. The boat made soft ripples in the water as the General carefully climbed in. He picked up the second oar and signalled Finn to start rowing.

As soon as the boat passed underneath the jutting boardwalk, Ella placed her hand in the air, telling them to stop. One of the soldiers had walked to the edge to relieve himself, with the spray of urine only just missing the boat. He swayed on the spot for a moment, almost threatening to fall into the sea. Another soldier called out to him, which brought the first back to his senses. "Hey, Roland. We've got a live one here! She's really feisty too."

"Just how I like 'em," the man whispered to himself. He buttoned himself back up and returned to the burning slum. It was only when Ella heard the woman's protesting screams that she reluctantly dropped her hand to signal for Martine and Finn to row on.

"I know that must have been hard for you," Martine said to Ella a while later, noticing a mixture of sadness and anger on her face. "There was nothing we could have done for the woman. Towns get sacked. That is an unfortunate consequence of war."

"Did it happen during your time in the militia, sir?" Ella asked.

"Yes...it did." He said nothing else, instead looking out to the horizon.

Ella thought his answer strange, but knew not to intrude further. The first time she had visited the General's office, she had noticed a small black and white photograph on his desk of a young woman. Ella had no idea who the woman was, but knew she must have been close to Martine, judging by the well-worn sides of the gold frame. Was Martine thinking about the woman at this moment? She thought he might be.

Hugging the jagged coast, the group soon saw the outline of the overhanging cliffs in the distance. Away from the town, the wind had now picked up, making a whooshing sound as the water rocked the boat back and forth. Martine pointed towards a large gap in the cliff face and eagerly rowed towards it. Both he and Finn had to fight the current to stop the boat smashing into the rocks at the entrance to the cavern, using every last ounce of strength to steady the boat. Once inside, he fished into his jacket pocket and held up his cigarette lighter. It didn't give off much light, but it was better than nothing.

The cave was damp and cool. Ella stared upwards in wonder, as the light revealed beautiful and mysterious yellow limestone stalactite formations hanging aimlessly from the ceiling. Razor sharp to the touch, Martine deliberately slowed the pace down as they navigated their way through the maze.

"They must be thousands of years old," Ella remarked, pointing to the glistening rocks. "I've never seen anything like it."

"Hundreds of thousands of years old," Martine corrected. "This cave was formed long before humans, elves or dwarves walked the planet."

Old and beautiful as they were, Finn gulped at the sight. The formations reminded him of harpoons, all of the time threatening to fall down on him and slice his head in two. He crossed everything that he could, breathing a sigh of relief as the cave opened up above them once more.

"Pull up here, Finn," Martine said, shining the flame towards the left hand wall. "If I remember right, there is a small passageway that will lead us to a ladder." He ordered Percy to remain with the boat. "If God is with us, we shall be able to access the dungeons from there."

'Hold steady, Leonhard,' Ella thought, closing her eyes. *'We're coming for you!'*

The elf woke from a slumber, as several drops of water fell from the ceiling. Shaking his head, he surveyed the prison cell, trying to return his mind to the present. The darkness made it difficult to see, save for a shaft of light from the corridor that outlined the weathered bars. The dungeon stank of stale body odour, dirt and waste matter. Despite his predicament, Leonhard had attempted to pray to his Elf gods, like he did every evening. Yet, the noise emerging out of the packed cells meant he couldn't concentrate and finally gave up on it.

Salamander had been thrown in the opposite cell to him, but looking out of the iron bars now, it was empty. Leonhard had no doubts that the former mercenary was above with the man he had called Rufus, trying to save his own skin.

'Salamander, you fool,' he thought bitterly. *'You didn't have a clue what you were getting yourself into.'*

The man had clearly asked for Salamander to bring Leonhard's father to him. Why? Was it linked to his sudden disappearance? Leonhard had lied to him that he wasn't Ruven Solveig's son, but he knew that the truth would come out somehow. What did they mean to do to him?

He knew it had only been a matter of hours since he had been locked up, but time seemed to have almost stopped. His stomach gave out a large groan, reminding him that he hadn't had anything to eat or drink since this morning. He could still taste the coppery tang of his own blood from where Salamander had struck him across the face.

The clinking of keys in the distance brought him to his senses. He got up stiffly from the soaking wet stone floor and looked out at the dimly lit corridor. Prisoners were calling out with groans and pleading screams to the approaching guards, only to be beaten back with truncheons for their troubles. Stopping outside Leonhard's cell, an oafish guard unlocked the door and swung it open forcefully. The man known as Rufus entered first, his face still strangely covered, whilst a guard remained outside. Salamander stood rather pensively at his side, looking anywhere but the elf. He still wore his Northwood academy jacket, but it was dirtier than before. It was clear that confinement had dented Salamander's pride.

"I am Captain Rufus Salt of the Focean Grand Army," the man said bluntly. "Salamander insists you are Ruven Solveig's son. Do you deny it?"

Leonhard was eager to find out what happened to his father, but didn't trust the man would tell the truth.

"I do," he said back sharply. "So you better let me go."

Rufus gave no indication whether he believed Leonhard or not. "I am not going to do that just yet," he said, with an emotionless laugh. "Salamander has asked for proof that 'he' is telling the truth."

Now wearing leather gloves that matched his coat, Rufus acknowledged the guard posted outside, who in turn, handed Salamander a small rusty scalpel and a copper petri dish.

"Take off your belt, Leonhard," Salamander said.

Sweat trickled down Leonhard's back at the sight of the knife. He licked his parched lips nervously. "Why should I?" he said finally.

Although Salamander's hard face remained, Leonhard noticed the man's eyes were anxious and skittish.

'He's just as scared as me,' he realised. Rufus stepped aside as the guard entered the cell and pushed Leonhard hard against the stone wall.

"What are you doing?" Leonhard cried out. The contact with the wall drew a sharp pain between his shoulder blades. He tried to wriggle free of the guard's grip, but the man was too strong.

"I am doing what needs to be done," Salamander whispered back. He undid Leonhard's belt with force and tied it tightly around his left arm, constricting the flow of blood. He then drew the scalpel swiftly across Leonhard's hand, catching the flow of blood with the dish.

It was a stinging pain like Leonhard had never experienced, but he gritted his teeth together bravely.

'I'm not going to give you the pleasure of hearing me scream,' he promised himself. *'I can do that at least.'*

Nevertheless, watching the dish turn crimson, the old Salamander seemed to return.

"I guess you tree huggers do bleed the same colour as us," he remarked with a smirk. Satisfied that he had taken enough of Leonhard's blood, he passed the dish carefully over to Rufus.

The captain nodded his head in approval. "For your sake, Salamander, I hope this works. Bind the wound. If the Sorceress is to strengthen, we will surely need more of the elf's blood."

Leonhard collapsed to the ground, feeling lightheaded and sick at the rapid loss of blood. "The Sorceress..?"

Salamander didn't answer. Looking at him pitifully, he tore off a piece of cuff from Leonhard's jacket and tied it around the wound. The man made a terrible job of it, as blood seeped through the makeshift bandage almost at once.

"Don't go anywhere now, Leonhard," Rufus said, mockingly. "We haven't finished with you yet!"

The guard let Salamander and the Captain leave the cell and slammed the door shut, locking it behind them.

Leonhard closed his eyes tight to relieve the stabbing pain that had started in his head. He knew it had only been a matter of minutes since he had drifted off, when a spine tingling, bloodcurdling scream awoke his senses. It was like nothing he had ever heard before. The scream was inhumane even to his ears. It was as sharp as a razor and cut through him like an ice-pick. He felt the vibrations ring in his head and travel through his body, freezing him to the wet ground. His eyes opened wide, paralyzed with fear.

"What in God's name was that?" a familiar female voice called out from further down the corridor.

"Whatever it was, it ain't good," another voice said. The sound of their voices were getting closer.

"Quickly now," a third said. This one sounded older and spoke with more authority. "Leonhard must be down here somewhere. Check every cell."

Leonhard tried to call out, but his voice was barely above a whisper. His hand still throbbed with pain and the blood had soaked through the bandage, forming a sticky pool on the floor. He tried to stand, but his legs gave way at once. He collapsed against the bars, slicing his hand even further against a jagged piece of coarse iron.

The three rescuers heard the crash and ran down the corridor instantly towards Leonhard's cell. They found the elf slumped against the wall, his whole body shaking as if he was experiencing a fit. He was clutching his left hand, crying in agony. General Martine leant back and kicked the lock with a relentless force. It took a further three blows for the cell door to creak open and break off its hinges with an almighty crash. Time would be short, as the remaining Focean soldiers would have heard the noise.

"Can you stand?" Martine shouted, rushing at Leonhard. The elf mumbled a confused answer, wincing in pain.

Finn and Ella each grabbed an arm, pulling him to his feet. They both looked at Martine in panic, aware of how much weaker their friend seemed. Another monstrous scream from above, this time even louder, caused the whole dungeon to shake violently. Pieces of chipped stone fell from the ceiling onto the three rescuers. The lanterns along the corridor abruptly blew out and shattered, sending shards of glass flying in all directions. It was as if they had stepped into the epicentre of an earthquake.

Hands shaking, Martine quickly reached for his lighter and led the way into the darkness past the anxious prisoners. The high pitched squeal had raised alarm bells immediately with him. He had heard the same scream many years before, and wished on his life never to hear it again. He knew what it could mean and it made him sick to the stomach. His cane made a clicking sound with the ground as he hastily limped towards the wooden trapdoor.

Leonhard could feel his strength sapping as Finn and Ella dragged him along the corridor. The walls closed in on him and it felt like he was wading through treacle. He was so tired that he could have easily just curled up on the stone floor and gone to sleep. He wanted to believe it had all been a terrible dream, expecting to wake up any moment in his warm bed in the academy dormitory.

Ella had to stop for a moment. Even though Leonhard must have only weighed around ten stone, her arm muscles ached and her heart pounded furiously. She also noticed Leonhard's eyes lose focus and blur over.

"He's losing consciousness, sir!" she shouted, leaning against a mouldy, damp covered wall. Spotting a leak in the roof, Ella gestured to Finn to hold

Leonhard under in the hope it would rouse him. She also took the chance to rip off the old bandage and soak the wound in the water. The palm looked puffy and swollen. Ella guessed it was the beginnings of an infection.

"He's a goner for sure!" one of the prisoners cackled loudly nearby. The General's light revealed a man with no nose and a face that was covered with tattoos. Clearly insane, he held the cell bars tightly and started to bash his head against them whilst chanting his crazy ramblings. When the man could take no more, he staggered back into the darkness and back out of sight.

Martine ignored the prisoner and threw Leonhard over his shoulder as if he was a sack of potatoes. Sweat running into his eyes, he ordered Ella to hold the trapdoor whilst he descended the ladder.

"Will he die, sir?" Finn said. The lad was visibly upset, as a single tear escaped one eye and trailed down his face.

"Not if I can help it. Now let's get out of here before we have company."

The last thing Leonhard could decipher was the reflections of light glistening wetly on the cave ceiling. He had been lowered into the boat and Finn shouted into his face, trying to keep him awake.

It was no good though; his best friend's voice seemed too far away. Leonhard's ears were muffled, as if he was deep underwater. His vision grew blurry and he could feel himself drifting between the realms of consciousness. He reached out his hand and felt Ella's warm touch. The darkness then took him.

Five

The captain came for Salamander at first light.

The former student at Northwood Academy, now turned rebel, had been dozing, albeit briefly. It took Salamander a moment to remember why he had been hauled into the room.

'The wretched elf has escaped,' he remembered, anger clouding his thoughts. *'And Salt had the damn nerve to blame me.'*

Salamander had quickly taken stock of his surroundings and wondered if the dark stone room had long ago been a guest room for the lord of the castle. It was bare, save for an empty bookshelf and fireplace, a brown and orange patterned rug in the middle and a dusty, moth eaten bed. Lying on it now, Captain Salt and three heavyset guards stood over Salamander with stern faces.

"Are you comfortable down there?" Salt asked. The Captain's flat, monotone voice made it hard to tell if he was attempting to be funny or not.

"Well, it sure is an improvement from the dungeon," Salamander replied. *'See Rufus, that's sarcasm for you!'*

Not wanting to quip with Salamander any longer, Salt gestured for the man to get up. "The Sorceress will see you now. She is not happy with you."

Salamander didn't have a clue what a 'Sorceress' was. He did guess that she held the power here though, judging by the way Salt had referred to her.

He considered the three guards at his side. The men held their bodies tentatively close and their weapons closer still, showing nervousness. Their eyes darted around the room, seemingly scared of their own shadows.

'They fear this Sorceress,' Salamander realised. *'Surely she can't be that bad. She is only a woman after all.'*

He wondered why Salt had failed to mention this so-called leader during their one and only meeting. It had been early evening and Salamander had been drinking alone in a tavern on Northwood's waterfront. Salt had silently pulled up a bar stool next to him and stated that he knew everything about him.

"Is that right?" Salamander had asked him back. "What do you know about me then?"

Salt knew that Salamander's alcoholic father had constantly beaten him to a bloody pulp in his youth. He also knew that, contrary to the official report blaming his mother, it was a teenage Salamander who had lit the match that burnt their house down, finally ridding himself of his evil father once and for all. And despite General Martine presumably feeling sorry for the homeless boy and enlisting him at Northwood's academy at the age of fourteen, Salt knew Salamander was looking to get back at Martine for not giving him an instructor job at the academy for the forthcoming year.

As he heard his life being spelled out to him in a matter of a few sentences, Salamander looked down at his whisky tumbler. He had drunk at least four measures of the spirit and was now starting to feel slightly worse for wear. He wondered if this strange man was just a figment of his imagination, reminding him of his failure in life.

"Why do you dress like that?" he had asked Salt, curiously referring to the black veil that covered the man's face.

The man had ignored the question. Instead, Salt told him he was looking for an elf named Ruven Solveig and tasked Salamander in finding him.

"He is an old friend of your General," he had said, oddly licking his lips in anticipation.

"Why should I help you?" Salamander had said, knocking back his whisky. It was the cheap stuff that burned the back of your throat, perfect for drowning your sorrows with.

"Think of me as a talent spotter. I hear you have talent, Salamander. In return for your favour, I will offer you a place in the Focean Grand Army."

Salamander knew it was an offer he couldn't refuse. After this coming year, he would be forced to leave the academy and had nowhere to go. This man was offering him a future and more importantly, a purpose in life.

The morning before he had been due to set off to Ilsthyr to kidnap the elf, he received a letter from Salt, telling him that Solveig had disappeared and the plan had now changed.

Find him! the letter had demanded. *'I will not waste any men whilst you search for him. I will be waiting at Sleima's castle in one week's time.'*

Salamander had ripped up the letter in a mad fury. Not only had he found Salt's tone insulting, he didn't fancy trapping across a country he had little knowledge of. The elf could literally be anywhere in Terra, or he might have even travelled to another continent.

He had spent the rest of the day in his dormitory, trying to figure out a new plan, when suddenly, it came to him. He would use Xai, the academy field operative to get what he wanted. Salamander had been secretly seeing the woman for the best part of two months and she had begun to adore him. She nagged him constantly to make their relationship official, something which Martine would not approve of. In his book, academy staff sleeping with students was definitely a sackable offence.

"I need you to persuade Martine to let me lead the next mission," Salamander had said, visiting Xai in her staff quarters. Staff members who didn't live in Northwood town would stay on site during term time and return home in the holidays.

Giving her what she wanted, she had agreed that Salamander would make a great leader.

"I know Francis has been thinking about it for a while," she had said, red faced from their rapid intercourse. "I'm sure a word in the ear from me would convince him."

He had also stressed to Xai that he wanted a handful of newly qualified recruits in his team. "For example, I hear the elf has just passed his practical exam. What is his name again?"

"Leonhard Solveig," she said at once.

"That's it. If I show the General that I can lead a group of students effectively, he might overturn his decision to make me an instructor."

He had known his next sentence would seal the deal, so he took his time and gently stroked her cherry brown hair. "Then there would be no need to carry on seeing each other in secret."

The plan had almost worked a treat. Now Leonhard had escaped from the dungeon, Salamander was being led to an uncertain fate.

With their tough, golden armour clinking behind him, the three guards led Salamander through a series of dark, twisting corridors and out onto a wooden bridge that rose high above the castle's central courtyard. Beyond the parapets, a faint yellow lined the horizon.

He halted his progress and looked towards the edge of the bridge. If he were to jump now, it would be a fall of over a hundred metres to the bottom of the courtyard. Death would be almost certain. It would be quick and relatively painless.

'For sure, it's a coward's way out, but it will be better than what the Sorceress has got lined up for me.'

Turning his body towards the edge, the guards behind him saw what their prisoner was about to do and quickly blocked his path with their tall, silver spears. The moment to jump had been and gone.

"Don't even think about it," Rufus said. With his gloved hand, he pointed to the other side of the castle that was partly in ruins. "The Sorceress would not have been pleased if you had died before she had a chance to meet you."

The ceilings in the left hand side of Sleima's castle were noticeably lower than the far side. Salamander had to duck to stop himself hitting his head on the black beams that lined the corridor. Salt stopped outside a heavy oak door and rapped three times with his fist. The noise reverberated around him. Satisfied that he had permission to enter, he twisted the door and led Salamander inside.

The icy cold temperature of the room hit Salamander instantly. He shivered, clutching his jacket closer. The outline of the old guest room was shaded, with the curtains drawn across and the lanterns all dark. He almost choked on the smell of rotting flesh. Death was in this room and he was about to meet it.

Rufus crept slowly forward and went to his knees. "My lady," he whispered, towards the end of the room. "I have brought you the man you wish to speak to."

At first, there was only silence. The atmosphere in the dark room was disquieting and unnerving. It was a relief to Salamander that the guards hushed breathing signified that they also felt the same as him.

He turned and looked behind. The door to the corridor was slightly ajar, with an outline of light highlighting the frame. He thought to try and overpower the guards and attempt to escape from the castle. From the noises he had heard last night, he knew that many of the guards were hungover following last night's pillaging of the town.

As if his mind was being read, the door slammed shut by itself.

"Bring him closer," a voice called out in the darkness.

The strained sound that emerged from the Sorceress's throat was nothing more than a croak. Salamander had not heard anyone speak in that way before. He suddenly felt fifteen years younger, as if he was back at his mother and father's house. The awful memory of his childhood made him shudder.

Timidly, the guards led him to the centre of the room. He could see Rufus on his knees, so he knew it would be wise to do the same.

"My lady," Salamander spoke to the blackness, his voice sounding incredibly weak and childish. "It is a pleasure to meet you. My name is Salamander Rourke." He then felt he should say something else. "I...err....am at your service."

From the corner of the room, the sound of bare flesh on stone grew closer until a black figure appeared in front of him. Salamander had to hold his breath and pinch his nose as the decaying smell suffocated his senses.

"My lady, it is not wise for you to be out of your bed," Rufus pleaded. "You are too weak."

"Nonsense!" the Sorceress replied in a biting tone. "I want to look at the man in the eye and ask him why he let the young elf escape."

As she leaned closer, Salamander saw her decomposing face for the first time and silently screamed in horror. Her skin was milk white and hollow. The Sorceress's nose and her right cheek had decayed completely to reveal the sinewy tissue and yellow bone underneath. Her hair was fine and brittle and her eye sockets were empty. A sickening yellow and green liquid dripped from her right ear and ran down her veiny neck.

'Dear God, I am talking to a corpse,' Salamander realised. He felt his ginger hair stick to his scalp and his body became paralysed with fear. Thankfully, she wore a nightgown that hid away the rest of the nightmare. As she breathed into Salamander's face, he had to turn away from her foul breath.

"My lady, we discovered a small trapdoor in the dungeons that led to a network of caves underneath the castle," Salt said. "We think the elf had assistance from General Francis Martine of the Northwood Academy."

"You knew?" the Sorceress asked Salamander, pointing an accusing finger.

Salamander forced himself to look at her rotting face. It was an image that he knew he could never forget for as long as he lived, however long that may be. "I had no idea!" he said sharply, rising to his feet. His voice rose with his temper. "Why would I bring him to you and then just let him escape? You should be blaming your captain for leaving the castle poorly manned, not me."

For a short time, the Sorceress stood still as a statue. It was as she raised her thin arms above her head that Salamander felt a tightness in his throat. It was as if his voice box was being crushed and his gullet was on fire. He crashed to the floor in a tremendous pain and clawed at his throat for air. As his life started to slip away, the dark room began to spin.

"Shall I kill him, Rufus?" she asked calmly, her jaw clicking up and down as she spoke.

Rufus stood over Salamander with his arms crossed, contemplating his next move. He was enjoying watching the man squirm and plead for his life. To Salt, it reinforced the power he now had. All of the risks and his own personal sacrifice had been worth it. Now he had the information he needed and once the Sorceress regained her full power, Focea would surely be untouchable. Carefully taking off his black veil, the cool air prickled his pasty skin. Doing this in the daylight would cause his skin to blister due to having spent so much of his life underground, but with the curtains drawn across, it was safe enough here.

"We will proceed as planned," he told her, inhaling in a deep breath. He knew he could use Salamander in the forthcoming campaign. And if he didn't, he would kill the former Northwood student himself. "Release him, my lady. Let him live for another day at least."

Six

The journey back to the ship had been relatively uneventful. The Focean soldiers had burnt Sleima's slums to the ground and started pillaging the town proper, allowing General Martine and Finn to row all the way past the pier and to the beach on the other side without being seen. Once on board, Martine had immediately rebandaged Leonhard's wound tightly to restrict the blood flow and placed him upstairs in Hobbs's cabin. Much like the captain himself, the bed was scruffy and the sheets definitely hadn't been changed for over a year. There were maps and newspapers strewn all over the desk, with the rubbish bin full of crisp packets and cigarette boxes.

"I have just spent half an hour tidying your cabin up, Hobbs," Martine said, walking into the control room. Francis Martine lived his life by order and it riled him that not everybody followed the same rules. "What do I pay you for?"

The captain barely lifted his head in acknowledgement. He wore the same dirty blue and white striped t-shirt that he always did. Looking out at the vast, inky black ocean beyond the glass window, Hobbs made steady turns of the wooden wheel with his callused hands. A mug of tea was at his side, with the liquid swaying with the movement of the ship.

"I thought you paid me for navigating this ship, Francis," he replied. The man turned and a wry smile twisted his lips. "I don't usually give my bed up that easily."

Martine ignored Hobbs's wit. He had worked with the man long enough to understand his dry sense of humour.

"How far now until we reach Northwood?" he asked gloomily.

"Another thirty miles or so. We should arrive before dawn." Hobbs picked up his drink and studied him for a moment over the rim of his mug. "What happened back there?"

Although Martine had known Hobbs for a long time, he first wanted to get back and debrief Xai and Vincenza Van Zandt, the academy's vice-General. There would be a lot to talk about and discuss. Only when a plan of action was formulated would he then consult Hobbs.

"Something bad," he said vaguely, leaving the control room.

Tired of the awkward silence between Finn and Percy below deck, Ella decided she would check on Leonhard. Climbing the ladder, the light from the lantern showed a solitary figure standing alone on the deck and braving the gusty wind. It was only when Ella got closer that she realised it was Xai. Her hair blew in all directions and tears coursed her cheeks.

"What's wrong?" Ella asked her.

Hearing her voice, Xai removed a tissue from her pocket and swiftly wiped away the tears. "Oh, hello," she said, smiling sadly. "I was just thinking, that's all."

Ella had always admired Xai and Vincenza for rising high in the academy in what was largely a man's world. She hoped that she could follow a similar path once her tutorship programme was up. "Do you want to talk?" she asked.

Xai said nothing for a moment, only staring ahead. Again, tears filled her eyes and this time, her lower lip trembled. "What do you think will happen to Salamander?"

Hearing his name had caught Ella by surprise. It then came to her why Xai was asking the question. "Are you in love with him?"

Xai didn't flinch and there was to be no denial in her voice. She glanced behind her, ensuring no one was overhearing. "If you must know, we've been seeing each other for a few months." She pushed herself up from the railings and repeated to Ella her first question.

"I guess that depends on what Salamander decides to do next," Ella remarked. She knew the woman would take it hard, but there was no point in sugar coating the issue. "He disobeyed General Martine's orders and put his colleague's life in danger. If he returns to Northwood, the General will place him under arrest for treachery. He will be tried under jurisdiction at the county court and sentenced to prison...or maybe executed."

With a sinking feeling, Xai understood. "I...I just wish I could see him one more time. Just to ask him, you know, why he did what he did."

'He betrayed us because he is selfish and cruel,' Ella mused. *'He doesn't care about you, nor anyone else for that matter. The man is a wretched snake and deserves what comes to him.'*

She had to bite her lip to stop her thoughts spilling out. She also had to hold back a laugh, which she knew would have been entirely inappropriate in the current situation.

"Did you have any idea what he was planning?" she asked.

"None, I swear. The only thing he asked of me was to talk to Francis about him leading the next mission and to put forward Leonhard's name." Her watery eyes suddenly bulged with alarm. "Please don't tell the General about any of this, Ella, I beg you!"

Ella grabbed Xai's arm to reassure her. Yes, she had made a stupid mistake, but the woman was in love. It was clear that she had no part in Salamander's plan.

"I won't," she promised. "You have my word."

Ella then retreated upstairs to the captain's cabin, closing the door behind her. Martine had taken off Leonhard's jacket and put the bed covers over the elf to keep him warm. She went over and placed a hand on Leonhard's forehead to check his temperature. His skin was clammy and warm to the touch. Colour had returned to his cheeks. She watched his chest rise up and down. Thankfully, Leonhard's breathing seemed normal.

She reached for a tissue and wiped the drool away that had crusted on one corner of his mouth. Ella hoped and prayed that the academy's doctor, Juliette Randowski, would be able to wake him.

"I'm sorry for being such a bitch to you," she whispered into his ear, hoping somehow he could hear her voice. "I know now that you were only trying to help me. Come back to me, please."

She leant in, intending to kiss him on the lips, when the deep blast of a horn startled her. The ship had arrived back at Northwood.

Northwood's harbour was quiet, except for several bleary-eyed fishermen loading their equipment into their small fishing boats. A large red tugboat stood motionless in a dry dock, held between the rocky confines of the basin. At the side of the narrow timber beamed promenade stood an attractive looking pavilion building, which regularly hosted light entertainment for Northwood's residents. Making their way down the pier, General Martine spotted Vice-General Vincenza Van Zandt waiting at the far side. She had been perching on the bonnet of a long six wheeled white saloon car, which contained a metal grill at the front and reflective silver alloys. Noticing the mercenaries carrying Leonhard on a stretcher, the short haired muscular woman took off her goggles that she seemed to always wear and straightened immediately.

"How bad is it?" she asked Martine, opening both of the rear doors.

"He has lost a lot of blood," the General replied, placing the stretcher on the rear leather seats. "We need to get him to the infirmary as soon as possible." As he and Xai climbed in the front seats, Martine instructed Finn, Ella and Percy to catch the trolley bus that serviced the school with the town. The car made its way along the wharf and out of sight, heading towards the towering academy in the far distance.

"But the buses aren't running yet," Percy remarked. He looked down at his watch, which told him they would need to wait an hour and a half before the first one left the station. "I guess we have a long walk ahead of us."

"Not for me," Finn said, stretching out. "I think I will stop by my Mum's place for some grub."

Ella looked almost appalled that somebody could eat at a time like this. "Well you better head back soon," she said sternly. "We need to be there when Leonhard wakes up!"

As Finn promised he would be, Ella and Percy started their long walk towards the academy. The building had been built on a separate island to the town, connected by a long arched stone bridge. The tarmac was wide enough for motor vehicles and the buses to run side by side, as well as having a designated pedestrian walkway. Finn had walked it many times before. He knew it would take them both at least three quarters of an hour before they arrived back.

He passed the closed shops on the waterfront and climbed up an elevated walkway that rose above the market street. Underneath him, the town was starting to awaken as stall holders were busy unpacking their wares ready for the weekly market day. The streets would soon be heaving with people. Finn loved the hustle and bustle of market day; the laughter, bartering and the wide variety of people all added to a carnival atmosphere. He was extremely proud to call Northwood his home.

Sitting in the middle of a vast ocean, Northwood's mayor had come up with an ingenious way to use the resources at its disposal and turn it into energy; hydroelectricity and wind power. A semi-circular dam and a generator had been situated five miles out to sea, with power lines and pipes running under water and onto the surface, snaking their way through the town. Steel wind turbines had also been built, allowing Northwood to become entirely self-sufficient. It had certainly made the town unique in that the majority of towns and cities on the western side of Terra still relied on burning fossil fuels for their energy. The building project, along with the growth of the shipbuilding industry and the building of the academy had transformed Northwood from a sleepy fishing village to a bustling hub, all in the space of a few years.

Using a well-used shortcut through the premises of a factory, Finn used his body to slide between two of the rust coloured pipes. Every couple of minutes, steam shot out of the valves, so Finn had to be quick to avoid getting sprayed with it. He had played there many times with his friends as a child, which had often resulted in the factory owner chasing them away for causing too much noise.

He was out of breath by the time he had climbed the hill to his mother's place in the heart of the residential zone. To cope with the growing population, many of Northwood's residents lived in back to back terraces, due to a lack of space on the island. They were cramped, often noisy and up to fourteen houses shared an inner courtyard, which contained wash houses and privies. Finn had actually been amazed when he was told he and Leonhard had their own en-suite facilities at the academy and their washing was to be done for them.

As the day started to reveal a slate grey sky, the street lights above Finn's head flickered off. His mother's place stood out from the rest of the street for having been built with multi-coloured bricks. He took the sweat stained bandana off his forehead and rapped his fist on the green door.

At once, heavy footsteps descended the stairwell. Smiling brightly, Finn's mother placed her arms around her son and squeezed him tightly. Facially, she was very similar to her son, with a short sharp nose and high cheekbones.

"My sweet boy, it is so good to see you!" she exclaimed. She studied him closely, placing her hands on her wide hips. "You've grown since I last saw you, you know!"

"But Mum, it's only been a fortnight," Finn said.

Yet, he realised she must have been telling the truth as he had to stoop to avoid hitting his forehead on the low ceiling. He saw that his mother had her black and white train conductor's uniform on, ready for work.

"What time do you start?"

"Not for another two hours, love. Let me make you some breakfast and you can tell me all about how your first mission went."

Finn took a seat at the table and took his jacket off. He had always been sure the table had been converted from an old ship's chest, judging by the gold lock in the middle and the studs on each side. He then noticed the living room looked somewhat different. It then came to him that the walls had been pasted with new wallpaper, showing a bright, floral design.

His mother cooked Finn up a hearty meal, consisting of kippers, sausages and a poached egg. He ate it rapidly and proceeded to tell his mother about the mission, starting with Salamander's deception.

"Those Rourke's have always been a bad bunch," Ms Walker said, applying red lipstick to her face in front of a small, circular mirror. "I know his father met a violent end, but from what I heard about him, he deserved it."

She had also made an effort with her greying hair, having brushed and curled it tightly. Coupled with her pungent perfume, it made Finn wonder if his mother was trying to catch the attention of an admirer at the train station.

"We had to rescue Leonhard from the castle," Finn continued. "He's unconscious, Mum."

Ms Walker could see the dejection on her son's face. She hadn't quite believed her son when he had informed her that Francis Martine had recruited an elf to the academy. An elf in Northwood! What were the chances of that?

She was even more surprised, and at first a little worried when the General told her Finn would be sharing a room with him. Her fears were quickly doused when she met Leonhard for the first time. He seemed friendly and polite, if a little shy. She was ultimately relieved that her son had finally made a friend who seemed sensible after years of mixing with the wrong crowd at school.

"I'm sure he will make a full recovery," she eventually said, warmly placing her hand in his. "That Doctor Randowski is one of the best in the business."

Finn had been on the infirmary treatment table several times himself and had suffered the wrath of the Doctor. Juliette Randowski was a stern woman who scalded students for simple minor cuts and bruises. For being knocked unconscious, Finn knew Leonhard would feel her full indignation when he woke up.

His eyes suddenly felt heavy. He didn't know if it was the effects of the large breakfast or the heat from the fire that was blazing away in the corner, but he felt like he couldn't keep awake. In a matter of moments, he found himself dozing face first on the table.

It was the turning of a door handle that woke Finn. He slowly put his glasses on and waited for his eyes to regain focus. Somehow, he had made his way upstairs into his old bedroom. Posters of his old Reno Racers heroes still adorned the walls, as if he was ten years old all over again.

'Am I dreaming?' he wondered, pulling the covers over him to keep off the chill of the room.

He sat up straight and looked out of the small, rectangular window. It was pitch black outside.

"You're finally awake," his mother said, leaning against the doorframe. She had changed out of her conductor's uniform and was now wearing a sky blue dressing gown, her hair dripping wet.

"How long have I been asleep?" Finn asked, rubbing the sleep from his eyes.

"Thirteen hours, give or take."

"Christ, thirteen hours!" Finn didn't realise how tired he was. "Why did you not wake me?"

"You looked peaky when you arrived. I thought it would be better to let you rest."

Finn threw the bed covers off in a panic and quickly stood up.

"I need to get back to the academy. Leonhard might have woken up! General Martine probably wanted to see me!" Suddenly feeling stressed inside, he searched the room for his dormitory keys and wallet, only to find them both nestled deep inside his trouser pocket.

"Stay here tonight," Ms Walker said, doing her best to calm her son down. "You can leave first thing tomorrow."

Finn looked at his watch in disbelief. It was a little after nine o'clock. If he hurried, there would still be time to catch the last shuttle bus to the academy. He refused her invitation and kissed his disappointed mother goodnight, running downstairs into the cool, crisp evening.

With the stale aroma of sweat clinging to his clothes, Finn decided he would grab a shower as soon as he got back to his room. He paced down his mother's street in a flash and nearly bumped straight into the crowd of people gathered on the corner. They stood, buzzing like a swarm of flies, all mesmerized by something in the sky. Flexing his elbows out to disperse the crowd, a tug on Finn's left thigh halted his progress.

"What do you think it means, laddie?" a grey haired woman asked him, sitting in a wheelchair. She stared at him behind thick rimmed glasses, waiting for an answer. It was one which Finn didn't have time for and he decided to ignore her.

"I was asking you a question, son," she persisted, pulling at his arm. "What does it mean?"

He didn't have a clue what the mad woman was on about. Thinking he had possibly walked into the middle of one of those crazy sects he often read about in the newspapers, he glanced nonchalantly up at the sky. What he saw next filled him with revulsion and horror. He blinked repeatedly, just to make sure his eyes weren't playing tricks on him and stared blankly back at the woman.

The moon had turned into a burning red fireball.

Seven

General Francis Martine was physically and emotionally drained. It had been an energy sapping day, having spent a large part of the day briefing Vincenza, Xai and the rest of the senior staff on the current situation. There had been frantic discussion on what the best course of action would be, but without having all of the facts, it was almost impossible to plan ahead.

'Leonhard will hopefully be able to shed more light once he wakes up,' he hoped.

Martine did know one thing though; somehow, the Sorceress had returned back to life from a certain death. The blood curdling scream had been too similar to the one he had heard all them years ago. And the return of Rufus Salt, a man he also thought dead, puzzled him greatly. Had his former friend and army colleague been directly involved with the Sorceress's resurrection? A mission which had seemed routine from the outset had now turned into something much more critical. It was the fear of not knowing what could happen next that worried Martine, with the anxiety spiralling through him in waves.

The General knew he should try and get some sleep, but his mind was racing faster than a steam train. With a cigarette lit in one hand and a glass of whisky in the other, he paced around his living quarters above the office, thinking over the events of the last twenty-four hours.

'Maybe music might help me think better,' he pondered.

With that in mind, he went over to the wooden cabinet in the corner of the room and opened the double doors. He had built up an extensive jazz record collection over the years, displayed naturally in alphabetical order. As soon as he dropped the needle on the outer groove of a record, the sweet notes of a saxophone washed over him, cleansing his thoughts. He sat back on his leather sofa and closed his eyes, trying to piece together the facts.

Martine had seen the deep cut on Leonhard's hand and knew what Salt had done.

'But the blood he took will only keep the Sorceress alive for a short time.'

Would the Focean force launch an assault to try and snatch the elf back? The only viable way they could reach Northwood would be by sea and Martine knew they didn't yet have a fleet.

He tried to place himself in his adversary's shoes and think about what he would do next if he had command of Salt's army? Like a light bulb being switched on in the centre of his brain, it suddenly all became clear.

'I would go after Ruven Solveig. Capturing Leonhard's father was undoubtedly the original plan, but the elf must have got wind of it and escaped Ilsthyr.'

Had Leonhard understood any of this before he had collapsed? Had he worked out who he was in relation to the Sorceress? Before Martine could input the number of the infirmary into his telephone dial, it rang out loudly, signifying an incoming call. He picked up the brass receiver to his ear, crossing his fingers for some good news.

"Sorry to disturb you so late, General," Dr Randowski started, her voice hushed so she wouldn't disturb her sleeping patients. "You asked me to ring you if there was any development."

Martine looked at his battered timepiece. Through the cracks of the glass, the two gold clock hands showed him it was a little after half past twelve.

"I was about to ring down myself," he reassured her. "How is Leonhard?"

The doctor bit back a yawn. "He feels groggy but he is awake. Shall I tell him you will see him tomorrow, sir?"

Martine knew that would be the most sensible course of action. Yet, he was desperate to speak to Leonhard and knew it could not wait.

"No," he said, I will be right down."

He had expected Dr Randowski to cut the call at that moment. She continued on the line however, her breathing hushed.

"There is also something else, Francis."

"Go on."

"I don't know how to say this. Have you looked outside recently?"

Martine gulped, anticipating the doctor's next words.

"Nurse Jackie noticed it on her rounds," she continued. "It is the moon, Francis. It has changed colour!"

His worst fears had now been confirmed. Martine was far from a religious man. Yet he knew the appearance of the 'devil moon' served as a warning, signifying that something bad had happened in the world or was about to happen in the near future.

'There can be no doubt now that the Sorceress is alive…'

He placed the telephone receiver down and grabbed his top hat from the rack. He descended the cast iron spiral staircase, heading towards the infirmary.

The approaching footsteps made Leonhard sit up in his bed. The room was cool, with a small breeze drifting in through the open window. His left hand had been bandaged up tight and stung when he tried to flex it. He ran his tongue around his mouth in a clockwise formation to try and get rid of the metallic taste of dried blood. As he reached for the glass of water at his bedside, two figures approached, one tall and thin and the other small and dumpy. For a horrible second, Leonhard believed he was back in Sleima's dungeons, until the coughing from a nearby student reassured him that he was safe and sound in Northwood's infirmary.

Strange enough, the two figures passed by his bed and walked towards the window at the end of the ward. The streak of light that reflected on the red and black chequered floor tiles struck Leonhard as odd. It was as if the sun was somehow still up. How could it be when it was the middle of the night? As the pair reached the glass window pane, the tall figure crouched and looked out at the sky. From his position, Leonhard couldn't see what they were staring at.

"Does this mean what I think it does?" he heard the Doctor whisper in a concerned voice.

"Yes. I believe she has returned."

"Holy Mother of God." Leonhard saw Dr Randowski make a mysterious sign across her chest.

The General placed a hand on her shoulder to comfort her and turned away. Leonhard couldn't help but notice that Martine had always walked with a limp from a previous injury. Tonight however, it was more pronounced and as his face came into view, he looked as if he had aged twenty years. He stood over Leonhard's bed and smiled a downcast smile.

"How is your hand, son?"

"It's quite swollen, but I can move it alright," Leonhard replied, showing the General the maze of bandages. "Why did I fall unconscious, sir?"

"Well, Leonhard, you lost a lot of blood. Dr Randowski has informed me that you also caught an infection in the hand, which she has treated." He pulled the curtains across slowly, shielding the pair from the other sleeping patients. He flicked the bedside light on, which emitted a faint yellow glow. "Can you remember what happened?"

Leonhard acknowledged that he did. He reached for another cup of water to smooth his hoarse voice.

"Salamander betrayed us, sir. He was working with a man named Rufus Salt." He saw the General's expression change. "Does the name mean anything to you?"

Martine clenched his fists and slumped down on a chair next to the hospital bed.

"Yes, I know him," he said vaguely. He didn't want to go into too much detail, not yet anyway. "Did he have a woman with him by any chance?"

Leonhard shook his head. "Not with him no. He did refer to one though, calling her 'The Sorceress.' Who is she?"

Martine raised his eyebrows and stared at his student closely. The elf's young blue eyes were full of wonder and of intrigue. Francis remembered what he was like at sixteen, starting his career in the military. He envied Leonhard for his youth.

"Does the name Leona mean anything to you?"

"No. Should it, sir?"

Martine seized a spare mug and poured himself some water from the chrome filter built into the wall. Running from the mains supply, each bed had its own water compartment. It was just another little extra that Martine had demanded from the builders of Northwood academy.

"The woman known as Leona was a Sorceress. She was especially powerful, capable of huge devastation."

He closed his eyes, remembering one particular mission he had led in the Akiran militia. With a small task force of twenty, Martine had been tasked with investigating the disappearance of a 'magic dweller' called Leona from the Circle Tower in the region of Norr. Martine had heard the rumours of the Tower being a grim and remote place, where cruel experiments would be conducted on the prisoners. What he saw there confounded his expectations; he could smell death in the air even before their boats reached the island. They found the tower a ruined mess, with charred bodies piled high amongst the rubble. It was clear to him that only one person had come out of it alive. He remembered vividly how the heavens opened as they attempted to leave the island, with lightning striking at their heels in a mad fury.

"Sir, are you alright? You're shaking."

Leonhard's voice returned Martine back to the present. "Was I?" He looked down at the floor, where a puddle of water from his mug had formed at his feet. "So, the Sorceress Leona was eventually defeated. But it appears she has now returned."

"Did they take my blood to resurrect this Leona, sir? Salt had instructed Salamander to bring my father instead."

Martine opened his mouth to speak and quickly closed it again. It reminded Leonhard of the action a fish would make when swimming underwater. "Yes, the Solveig blood would do that. That is because..."

Leonhard finished Martine's sentence for him. He knew what the General was about to say. He had his suspicions as soon as Salamander drew the blade across his left hand.

"She is related to me, isn't she?"

Martine inclined his head. There would be no point in denying it, not now. He was mad at Ruven Solveig for not telling his son sooner.

"Yes, I'm afraid she is. Leona is your Dad's sister."

For a while, Leonhard said nothing. He simply stared at the General in disbelief. Suddenly, his eyes flared.

"My father has no sister! I would have known if he had. The only Auntie I had was my Aunt Edwina on my mother's side and she died when I was younger!"

"I don't blame you for being mad," Martine said, holding his hands up. "I know it must be a shock to you, Leonhard. But all of the evidence aligns to the truth, right? Your father has disappeared because he knew Salt was coming for him."

"So he let me get taken instead? He didn't think to warn you?"

"No, he didn't. You must believe me, Leonhard."

Leonhard threw the bed sheets away and crawled to the far end of the bed.

"I don't have to do anything you say," he sneered with his back to the General. "Get out and leave me alone!"

"I know it's late and you must be tired. We will talk more in my office tomorrow."

"Get the fuck out! Now!"

Dr Randowski drew the curtains back, looking bemused.

"And just what is going on here?" she asked, holding a number of patient reports in her hand.

"It's nothing," Leonhard sneered back. "The General is just leaving. Aren't you, 'sir?'"

Martine thought about countering the response, but knew it was no good. Elves were stubborn by nature and that, coupled with the lack of sleep and the side effects of the morphine Leonhard was taking had created a raging cocktail of anger. There would be no change in his mood tonight, that was clear to see.

"Leonhard, you should apologise to the General at once," the Doctor said sharply.

"It's ok, Juliette," Martine said. "It is late. I will leave you both in peace."

He turned to Leonhard, who was looking directly at the ceiling above his bed. "Come and see me tomorrow, please. We need to talk about what happens next."

With no acknowledgment that Leonhard had heard, General Martine stepped away from the light with his head slumped down and stepped through the automatic infirmary doors.

Leonhard lay on his back, wide awake. Dr Randowski returned with a mop in her hand and began soaking up the water that had spilt from the General's mug. She did it silently, only briefly tutting at Leonhard for the language he had used. That was fine with him. He was so lost in his thoughts that he didn't feel like speaking to anybody else tonight.

He suddenly realised he was gripping the bed sheets tightly with his fists and released them at once.

'How can she be my auntie? My Father has never mentioned a woman called Leona in the family.'

Leonhard suddenly remembered the large family painting that hung proudly above the fireplace in his parents' house. Painted before he had even been born, a young Ruven and Elarie Solveig stood smiling, arm in arm. Leonhard's grandparents and his Aunt Edwina stood proudly behind them on a wooden walkway, with a plethora of pine trees in the background. At the bottom of the picture was an inscription; *'The Solveig Family; 1989.'* There had been no evidence of any woman called Leona in the family.

'My Grandmother would have wanted her portrait in the family picture, surely.'

Yet, Leonhard knew deep down that may not have been true. If the family knew of Leona's magic traits, they may have informed the authorities and had her taken away before the picture had been painted. Or someone may have done that for them. Elves were a suspicious race and wouldn't want anyone living in Ilsthyr that would upset the peace. Leonhard couldn't help feeling a little sorry for the woman, despite what she had become.

'They completely erased her from memory. It was like she didn't exist!' He was furious at both General Martine and his father for not telling him sooner.

He looked towards the end of the bed, where his bare feet were sticking out from under the covers. Dr Randowski had returned to her office near the entrance. The two other patients in the infirmary, a male and a female student, were both snoring softly. It would be dawn soon; the shadows of the night were already starting to break and turn the sky to a denim blue colour. Leonhard listened to the faint sound of the morning chorus in the distance and closed his eyes. His mind ached with confusion and he had so many unanswered questions. He concentrated slowly on his breathing and eventually drifted off to sleep.

Eight

The room was still dark when Leonhard opened his eyes. Awakening his senses, the first thing he noticed that was different was the change in temperature of the room. It had turned bitterly cold, so much so that he could see clouds of his own breath as he exhaled. The bed sheets gripped to his naked body like ice. The howling wind shook the curtains and through it, he could hear the sea crashing against the rocks. It wasn't only his hand that throbbed with pain; his whole body tingled as if needles had been inserted into every pore of his skin. His head and his body ached from the inside out. His mind was heavy and it was like peering through a cloud of smoke.

The room smelled awful and Leonhard was certain he was the cause of it. *'What has happened to me? I smell like I haven't bathed in years. Something is very wrong here!'*

A knock sounded at the door. He tried to speak but his throat had become so dry that no sound emerged. He held his left hand up to pull across the curtain and was horrified by what he saw. Nearly all of his skin had rotted away to leave the last resins of tissue and dirty yellow bone. He could clearly make out the metacarpal bones that connected his fingers to his wrist. Spying a maggot working its way up his decomposed arm made Leonhard heave. There was nothing in his stomach to come back up though, so all he could do was groan and pull the creature away from his arm. He hesitantly glanced under the covers to see if the rest of his body was in the same shape. Disheartened to him, it was.

There was another rasp on the door, this time louder, and the handle started to turn.

"My lady," a man called out. The flat humourless voice was familiar to Leonhard, but he couldn't place where he had heard it before. "Please accept my apologies for the disturbance. I wanted to tell you that all the preparations have been finished and we leave in the morning."

When he heard no response, the man moved closer, peering over him like a dark shadow. Only one man Leonhard knew wore a black veil; Rufus Salt. *What is he doing here? Has he come to take me away again? Also, why did he refer to me as 'my lady?'*

The man took off the mask and revealed a face that gave the impression of it being engulfed in bleach. It was clear to see Salt hadn't seen sunlight in years. Leonhard could see the network of purple veins that criss-crossed under his paper thin skin. His hairline had retreated all the way to the back of his mushroom shaped head. Yet, matted grey hair protruded wildly from his nostrils and ears.

"Is everything alright, my lady?" he whispered.

'Does everything look alright to you?' Leonhard scowled. The only reply he could muster was a harsh rattle. He felt his head shake on its own accord with an immediate stabbing pain at the centre of his brain. It was so excruciatingly painful that it felt as if his head was about to split in two. Something was inside, pulling at the wires. He wanted to cry out in agony, but from nowhere, another voice came out of his mouth.

"Something is inside me," it said slowly, the raspy voice as dry as a desert. If Salt was concerned, he didn't show it.

"I thought this might happen," the man said, holding out his long arms towards Leonhard's head. "Hold steady, my lady. This might hurt a bit." With Salt's glacial touch, Leonhard felt a strong pull on his chest and felt his body rising from the bed. As his form was squeezed through a dark vortex, he now floated above a castle. Rising higher still, he could see the whole town that surrounded it, ruined by fire and smoke. Leonhard thrashed his arms around, but his body seemed to be on auto-pilot. In no time at all, he had ventured as high as the stars and was about to crash into the Earth's atmosphere. He saw the bright glow above him and shielded his body for the inevitable impact. Leonhard screamed at the top of his lungs...

...and woke up with the sunlight streaming into his eyes. The bedding around him had been screwed up into a ball, damp with sweat. His heartbeat pounded in his ears and his cheeks felt hot and flushed. He sat up, feeling lightheaded, unable to understand what had just happened.

The female student across the ward stared at him with mild amusement. Her left leg had been suspended upwards, wrapped in bandages. The belt made an irritating squeaking sound whenever she moved her body. The nurse Leonhard knew as Jackie had just finished taking the woman's blood and came racing over with her medication trolley to Leonhard's bed.

"You woke with a start, hun," she said in her usual flirtatious tone.

If Dr Randowski came across as cold and stern, Nurse Jackie was anything but. She must have only been a couple of years older than Leonhard and acted as if she had the hots for the elf.

Leonhard wasn't a fool though. He had seen Jackie bat her eyelashes at other male students too and often wore low cut tops to work that revealed a little too much. He wondered why the Doctor hadn't told Nurse Jackie to dress more appropriately in the infirmary.

"It was just a bad dream," he replied, feeling dazed.

"I have good news for you, my sweet," said Jackie. "You are being discharged today! Tell me, how is your hand?"

With the nightmare still fresh in his mind, he had forgotten all about his actual injury. It still looked swollen and sore, but it didn't sting as much as yesterday. Relieved to see all of his skin intact and of a normal colour, he moved his hand up and down to show her it was in working order.

Nurse Jackie leant over his bed to inspect the bandage. Her chest was so close to his face that he almost choked on her perfume. It would have been sure easier for her to walk around the other side, that much he knew.

"The bandage looks dry," she said cheerfully. "I will get Dr Randowski to write the report up and then you're free to go. Why don't you get showered and dressed and I will sort you out some breakfast?"

Leonhard did as he was asked, relieved to be clear of the nurse. He took the freshly washed uniform that had been hung up beside his bed and staggered conspicuously towards the bathroom.

His first shower since the mission made him want to stay under the hot water forever. He felt instantly refreshed. His breakfast, consisting of a bowl of honey porridge, a yogurt and a banana was waiting for him at the bedside table on his return.

The day was cast in brilliant sunshine. Gazing out of the window, Leonhard could see the peaks of the mountains that surrounded the academy in a natural bowl. Water forced its way through a ravine and descended past the mountain temple via an atmospheric waterfall into the lake below. He had spent many an hour fishing the lake in his spare time and he would also use the tall trees at the base of the mountains as target practise for his arrows. Being away from the bustling atmosphere of the academy made him relax and the trees reminded him of home. When Finn first became friends with Leonhard, he had also joined in, making a game of it to see who could get closest to the target. After fifteen consecutive losses, Finn eventually gave up and left Leonhard to practise by himself.

His mind returned sharply to the nightmare. He was under no illusion that he had taken the part of Sorceress Leona. Was it just a coincidence that he dreamed of her after his talk with the General or was it something more?

'It seemed so real. I could feel her trying to fight back.'

Finishing his breakfast, he decided to try and find Finn to tell him about his dream. They definitely had a lot to catch up on and maybe his friend could shed some light on recent events.

Leonhard signed the paperwork at the front desk and Dr Randowski gave him some ointment to put on his wound.

"It will leave a scar," she told him bluntly. Her tone suggested she still disapproved of his language from the previous night. Leonhard thanked her nonetheless and went through the sliding doors into the central plaza.

With its bronze coloured exterior, the academy had been built in a strange circular shape. All of its main facilities were situated on the ground floor, which included the library, cafe, infirmary, girls and boys dormitories, the practise yard, training arena and gymnasium. The eight low-ceilinged corridors all led back towards the bright central plaza, capped by its stunning skylight. A geometric patterned stairwell, complete with wrought iron and polished oak railings led to the students classrooms on the first floor, which could also be reached via a hydroelectric powered lift. General Martine's office and living quarters were positioned on the uppermost floor and could only be accessed by a special appointment.

Even if it had taken a while for Leonhard to adjust to the fast paced lifestyle and modern technologies that humans lived by, he had found the academy easy to navigate and follow. He glanced upwards at the brass clock hanging above. It had just gone nine o'clock. Finn would surely be tucking into his breakfast at this time, so Leonhard decided to head to the cafeteria.

Once there, he scanned the busy tables, but his friend was nowhere to be seen. He also looked around for Ella, but again, she wasn't there. Even though he had only just eaten, the smell of freshly cooked bacon made his stomach churn. He pulled a plastic tray from the rack and waited in the queue.

At once, Leonhard felt a heavy hand on his shoulder. Spinning around, Vice-General Vincenza stood behind him, her athletic arms folded across her chest. She had two round red marks around her eyes from where her goggles usually were.

"You've been discharged already, I see," she said, her face stern.

With her military demeanour very much intact, Leonhard found the woman slightly scary. He had been in her 'Art of Defence' classes for the last year and it was his least favourite subject. For some unknown reason, she repeatedly picked him when performing demonstrations to the class.

"I was looking for Finn, ma'am," Leonhard said. "Have you seen him?"

"Who?"

"Finn Walker. Medium height, curly black hair, glasses."

"Ah, him. No, I haven't. I have to come to collect you, though. The boss wants to see you in his office."

"Well if I'm honest, I don't really feel like talking to General Martine today."

The cafeteria had fallen so silent that Leonhard was sure he could hear a pin drop. The majority of students had stopped eating and were now listening in on their conversation. Vincenza didn't seem bothered by his challenge.

"We can do this the easy way or the hard way, Leonhard. Either way, you will come with me to his office."

Leonhard thought it would be unwise to cause a further spectacle, so he placed his tray back and reluctantly followed Vincenza back into the plaza.

Her regimental strides were so enormous that it took every last amount of Leonhard's energy to keep up. A group of students gathered outside the training area saluted as she went past, which she returned.

The open-planned nature of the academy meant a person could look up and follow the movement of the lift, as well as watching students and staff navigate the numerous wooden walkways that took them between the classrooms. Vincenza pressed the white backlit button to summon the water-powered lift and then used the hinge to slide open the scissor gate. Once inside, she hovered her finger above the second floor button and the carriage started its journey upwards once more.

Leonhard had only used the lift sparingly, opting to use the main stairwell out of habit. Unlike Finn, he was used to heights from his days growing up in Ilsthyr, so didn't mind the glass panelled floor showing him the distance they had travelled. The third time he had rode the lift, Leonhard had noticed a minus one floor button on the keypad below the ground floor option. To make the button active, a user would need to insert a key into the lock. "What is down there?" Leonhard had asked Martine inquisitively, not long after he had started at the academy.

"Nothing important," Martine said. "We use it mainly for storage, really." The General's lack of eye contact suggested to Leonhard he may not have been telling the whole truth.

The topic of the minus one floor had been a hot topic between him and Finn in the early days. Leonhard had thought it may have been an escape route, with a network of tunnels underground leading towards Northwood Town. Finn had offered something much more macabre. He thought the academy had been secretly built on top of an ancient burial ground. The reality was that they would never know without stealing the magic key.

"Don't be too hard on the General," Vincenza said, watching Leonhard with close scrutiny inside the lift.

Leonhard said nothing back, preferring to watch a group of students playing cards on the first floor walkway.

'If he cares that much for me, he would have told me about the Sorceress when I first started here.'

With a click clack noise ringing above their heads, the lift had arrived at the small waiting room outside Martine's office. Vincenza swung the gate open once more and let Leonhard step out first.

"Are you not coming in, ma'am?"

"He wants to see you alone. It seems you both have a lot to talk about."

She took the elevator down, leaving Leonhard staring intently at the General's office door. Part of him didn't want to go through it. He knew whatever he had learnt about his father's past was about to be turned on its head.

As his fingers found the door handle, it opened for him. Martine stood in the doorframe, dark shadows under his eyes from a lack of sleep.

"How long were you planning to stand there?" he asked. The corners of his lined mouth rose slightly as he attempted a weak smile.

"You wanted to see me, sir?" Leonhard said, a hard tone present in his voice. He wanted nothing more than to get this over and done with quickly.

The General urged the young elf to step into his office. It was a small room, with a blue and white patterned rug interrupting the wooden beamed floor. A wood burner had been positioned in the left hand corner and a twisting staircase led to Martine's living quarters above. The General moved over to the diminutive bay window that overlooked the vast expanses of the blue ocean. He gestured for Leonhard to sit down at his desk.

"I'd rather stand, sir."

"Suit yourself. I can see you're still angry with me." Martine came away from the window and pulled out his walnut coloured leather wingback chair from behind the desk. "I must say, I didn't realise elves used the 'f' word."

Had Leonhard swore at the General in his anger? He couldn't remember. All of a sudden, he felt guilty and took up the offered seat, softening his stance. "We have been known to use a lot more when provoked."

The silence between them lasted for over a minute. "So what do we do next?" Leonhard asked eventually. "Are we going after my father?"

"I agree that a visit to Ilsthyr might be a good place to start," Martine said. "Now I know that time is short, but I need you to understand the bigger picture. You need to know what happened before, Leonhard. All I ask is that you listen to what I have to say. Can you do that?"

Leonhard nodded. Finally, he might get some answers.

Martine drummed his fingers idly on the maple surface of the tabletop, searching his mind for a starting point. Telling his story would bring back a lot of bad memories, but the elf needed to hear it. He owed that much to him at least. The General inhaled deeply and began.

Nine

"I was born in the city of Akira to the west of Northwood. Have you heard of it, Leonhard?"

"Yes, sir. My father once told me it is the largest human city in the world. And also the dirtiest."

Martine couldn't argue with that. With Akira's centre bustling with industry, the plethora of factories in its centre pumped out a huge amount of smoke and gas, polluting the atmosphere. A thick layer of smog corrupted the streets, making the sky glow an eerie yellow. Akira's residents often wore white mouth guards when walking to protect their inhalation.

Below the surface was a shadow city called 'The Undercity.' Home to the Akira's destitute, it was a grim place rife with crime and desolation. Martine had always been told to stay away from there by his parents, but he never listened.

"I grew up in the shadow of the militia headquarters and would often see soldiers patrolling our neighbourhood," he continued. "I became engrossed by the stories they would tell me and signed up to the military as soon as I turned sixteen. I quickly became a good sword hand and was quick in my youth. I rose through the ranks and as the squadron's reputation grew, there was an increasing demand for our work outside of the city. We became mercenaries for hire, much like you are today. Then, as I hit my mid-twenties, something happened that turned my world on its head."

"The Sorceress?" Leonhard asked.

"Correct. The woman we both know as Leona repeatedly escaped any attempts to hold her in captivity. Slowly but surely, she grew in power and used her magic to influence the President of Norr, Jans Christensen, into making her his Vice-President. She would become his envoy, standing in on his behalf at diplomatic meetings and would speak with her own voice. He decided to coronate her in a grand ceremony to be held in the ancient city of Jarlstadt, Norr's capital. The Continental Congress knew what the woman was capable of and met in secret to formulate a strategy. It was King Luthai of Ilsthyr who first contacted our group."

"I see the look of surprise on your face, Leonhard. Forgive me for saying this, but this was in the days before Luthai became a fat old drunk. He was a respected member of the Congress and had planned the mission through meticulously. It would be a small team. "The smaller it is," he said to me, "the higher chance of success." As I had been chosen as the squadron leader, he asked me to select my best soldier and to travel to Ilsthyr for the brief. Do you know who I chose?"

"No, sir," Leonhard said.

"Rufus Salt."

For a moment, Leonhard was too stunned to say anything. "You knew him?" Just hearing his name again made him shudder.

"Even though I was his superior, we were good friends. Yes, he was sometimes brash in our missions, but his judgement and strength were usually second to none. Also, as he was born in Focea, I thought his knowledge of the land might come in handy."

He paused to light up a cigarette. As he breathed in the dirty tobacco, the end of the stick glowed bright orange.

"I don't think King Luthai trusted me entirely, not at that moment anyway. All he saw in me was a brash young man with nothing to lose. To assure him of mine and Rufus's loyalty, he ordered his best soldier to accompany us. Any guesses who that was?"

"My father?"

"Correct. Our mission would be to sneak into the ceremony and assassinate the Sorceress."

Turning his head to avoid inhaling the worst of the smoke, Leonhard furrowed his brow.

"You mean to say my father just went along with it?" he asked. "Leona was his sister, for heaven's sake! That's what 'you' told me anyway!"

"Of course, it must have been hard for Ruven, as it would be for anybody. Deep down, he knew what she had become and the threat she posed to Terra's peace. Besides, it was a direct order from his King, the one he had sworn to follow and protect to the grave. He wouldn't dare disobey him."

"Luthai gave us his favourite hunting rifle to use in the mission. I quickly handed it over to Rufus, knowing he was considerably more accurate with a pistol than me or your father. I don't know if it is the benefit of hindsight, but I saw something in Rufus's eyes at that point. It was like suddenly the weight of responsibility and the realisation of the mission's importance finally caught up with him. If only I had changed my mind about bringing Rufus, maybe things would have turned out differently..."

"Sir, the Rufus Salt you describe sounds completely different to the one I encountered," Leonhard said. "He wore a mask over his head to protect his face and he had strange marks on his skin. Do you really think it could be the same person?"

Martine considered his student's words. He got up stiffly and limped towards the bay window. A flock of birds flew past the roof of the academy in a V-shape and landed on the golden sands at the island's edge.

"Until yesterday, I thought he was dead. Killed by Leona. Instead, it seems as if he has sacrificed his physical health to resurrect the Sorceress."

"What happened next, sir?"

Martine turned around, still in a daze. "Hmm?"

"What happened when you left Ilsthyr?"

"Ah yes, of course. From there, we caught the train directly to Jarlstadt. We arrived the night before the ceremony was due to take place. The city was heaving. People had heard rumours of the Sorceress and had travelled far and wide to see if she was actually real. I immediately noticed the tight security, with Christensen's soldiers patrolling the streets in packs. It made me incredibly nervous. I thought it would be best for us to split up for the night, with my reasoning being that the mission could still go ahead if only one of us was captured."

"We spent the next day fine tuning the mission. We knew the evening's itinerary like the back of our hands. First of all, President Christensen would make a speech on the roof of his palace, announcing the Sorceress as part of his Government. There would then be a parade on an open top carriage through the city's streets. As it passed underneath the Presidential Arch, we would drop the iron gates, trapping the Sorceress inside. She would be a clear target for Rufus. The plan was almost perfect."

"Almost?" Leonhard asked. "I'm guessing something went wrong."

"You guess correctly," said Martine, returning to his seat. "The Sorceress had already planned ahead. As Christensen gave a typically long and overdramatic speech, she killed him outright in cold blood. We had just moved into position when we heard the commotion. The rest of the crowd carried on cheering as if nothing had happened. She had enchanted them, you see. They were blind to the actual truth."

"Promoting herself there and then to the Presidentship, she took her place in the vehicle and it travelled down the street towards the arch. Me and your father waited above in the control room, ready to pull the lever. I remember closing my eyes and waiting for his signal. We could hear the sound of the carriage getting closer and closer and then, well, there was only silence. We ran to the window overlooking the street and there she was, looking straight up at us both. Her expression...well, it scared the life out of me! It was a look of pure evil, I tell you. It wasn't only her though. The rest of the crowd gaped at us like statues, with their empty eyes and open mouths. The Sorceress's carriage then reversed back down the street. We quickly fled into the sewers below before her guards caught us."

"To be fair to Rufus, he stayed true to his word. We could hear his shots even as we retreated down the ladder. He fired them off like a man possessed. From what he told us later, she had deflected all but one of the bullets into the helpless crowd. The last one managed to wound her though, embedding itself in her shoulder."

"The sewers eventually led us out of the city. Rufus had already beaten us to the outskirts and waited for us at the highest hill with a wide grin on his face. He handed me a pair of binoculars and pointed in the direction of the north. At first, all I could see was the pre-dawn glow of Jarlstadt's skyline and the frosty plains beyond. I tinkered with the vision switch and found what he wanted us to see. It was the Sorceress fleeing from the city. Even from a distance, I could see the blood pouring from her wound."

"I urged Rufus to finish her off with the rifle, but he only shook his head at me. He told me she was too far out of range. I have never been totally clued up on the specifics of rifles, but to me, it looked the same distance as it had been from his sniper position back in the city. I do know though it was the first time he had refused an order from me. And...well, it wouldn't be the last."

"As we followed her trail north, the cliffs pressed close in around us. We had no choice but to follow the Sorceress through a dark forest. Thinking her lost, it was your father who eased my fears by scaling the tallest tree and spotting her on the far side of the forest. She had stopped to rest, but sneaking up on her was out of the question. She had summoned a hard protective shell to ward off any attackers. Clearly, the only thing to do was to rest for the night, with your father keeping watch. It had been a painfully long day and the mission had created a lot of nervous tension between us. I didn't realise how tired I was until I opened my eyes again and sunlight broke through the trees."

Martine bent forward and reached for the framed photograph on his desk. He peered at it longingly and turned it around for Leonhard to see.

"I expected to see Rufus sleeping beside the fire, yet he was nowhere to be seen." He tapped on the glass with his finger. "Instead, 'she' stood over me."

"Who is she?" Leonhard asked, regarding the young woman in the picture.

"Her name was Freya. I suppose she was what you'd call my childhood sweetheart. We were inseparable in our youth. She left Akira when I was twelve, venturing south with her parents. Age had only made her more beautiful, but I couldn't get over how little she was wearing. The only item that covered her body was a thin silk dress that came down to her ankles and she had travelled barefoot. Yet, her feet weren't dirty in the slightest. I then noticed a tattoo of a four pointed star on her right wrist. I learnt she had left her parents and joined a religious cult called 'The Blind Faith.' Naturally, I had never heard of them before, so I asked Freya why she was here and all alone. She told me that she sought the same thing we did; the Sorceress."

"It was then that Rufus and your father entered the clearing. I introduced her to them both and told them the same thing she told me. I could see the sceptical look on both of their faces. Tell me Leonhard, what do you know of the Elemental Crystals?"

"Sorry, sir," Leonhard said truthfully. "I've never heard of them."

"That's alright, I hadn't either. According to Freya, she had learnt there to be four crystals in the world that harvested all of the power and matter of the universe; fire, water, earth and ice. As you probably know, these are the four basic elements that are essential for life to exist. She told me that 'The Blind Faith' exists to cleanse the world of evil in God's way. With the location of the crystals only known to a select few, Freya had been instructed to find them, survive each guardian's trial set before her and harvest the crystal's divine power."

"Both me and Rufus were speechless. We had learnt the story of four crystals to be a myth, something that you would hear during a bedtime story. It was Rufus who spoke first, claiming that only weapons such as the one he held in his hand could stop Leona. Much to his annoyance, Freya informed us that she had attended the ceremony the previous night and had used a tiny amount of her magic gained from the crystals to place a hole in the Sorceress's protective shell, allowing one of Rufus's bullets to sneak through."

"Your father had remained quiet until then, but then spoke to back up Freya's beliefs. He informed us that he knew the Earth Crystal to be under the Temple of Odin in Ilsthyr and he had travelled underground several times with the King to see it."

Why do I not know any of this?' Leonhard wondered, biting back a hiss of frustration. *'There is so much that father never told me.'*

"Rufus regarded each of us like our heads were on backwards," General Martine continued. "He spat at my feet and started towards the edge of the clearing, cursing as he went. I tried to order him back, reminding him of the mission at hand and how Freya could be an asset to us, but he was gone. I could understand his behaviour in some ways. If I hadn't known Freya like I did, I would have thought her crazy too."

"By the time we had emerged from the woods, the Sorceress had left. Rufus had become only a speck in the distance, scampering north. We followed his route, with the weather turning colder all of the time. I asked Freya why Leona was travelling this way instead of heading south. She told us about a cave at the northernmost point of Norr that contained a fabled healing pool. She knew that the Sorceress would seek out this pool and tend to her wound before it was too late."

"We braved snowstorms, blizzards and even an avalanche at one point. It took a lot out of me and your father. Given Freya's lack of clothing, I often wondered how she kept herself alive through the freezing temperatures. She told me not to worry. The magic she had collected kept her warm inside. I just wish she could have shared some of the magic around! We became ever closer as we journeyed north, sharing stories and jokes like we were little children. Except this time, well, there was a sort of romantic chemistry between us. Have you ever been attracted to someone, Leonhard?"

Martine's question came completely out of the blue. It didn't feel right telling the General his feelings for Ella. "No, I haven't," he lied.

"Of course, you are still young," Martine said. "I can't explain how you feel, but when you meet 'the one', you will just know. Take my word for it."

"Anyway, your father would take himself off each evening to hunt for food. Sometimes he would be gone for hours on end. He was a man of few words but would always return with enough food to keep both our stomachs full. I say both as Freya hardly ate anything. The magic inside her meant she didn't need to eat or drink to stay alive."

"After a week of travelling, we arrived at a short distance from the entrance to the cave and camped for the evening. I hardly slept that night. I was worried what might happen to Freya when she came up against the Sorceress. Now she had only come back into my life, I desperately didn't want her to be taken away from me. I went for a stroll in the middle of the night to try and clear my head and spotted her leaving camp. She told me she needed to travel to a place called the Shimmering Isle to find one more crystal to complete her pilgrimage. I pleaded to go with her but she told me to remain with your father. I thought she might be gone for a few days, but the next morning, she had returned, ready to finish what she had started."

"I rose with the vain hope that maybe Rufus had killed the Sorceress for us. He had weakened Leona before, of course. Maybe with her defences down, a bullet might be all that was needed. That dream was shattered as soon as we entered the cave. I saw my old friend's body face down in the dirt. His rifle had been twisted in two and used to blow a hole his stomach. He had been a fool, but a brave fool nonetheless. Standing over his body, I felt a fury I had never felt before. We needed to kill her there and then."

"As expected, we found her by the pink glow of the healing pool. I sensed her evil voice inside my head, clouding my judgement. I can't exactly remember her words, but it made me crouch in pain. Your father felt the same too, cupping his head in his hands."

"Freya shouted over to the Sorceress with a voice louder than I thought was humanly possible. The cave shuddered around us, causing pieces of rock to fall away. As Freya began her battle, I detected a group of black creatures crawling along the cave ceiling. I had never seen anything like them before or have I since. They each looked like bats, but their bodies were jet black and about three times the size of a normal bat. The strangest thing I noticed is that they left no shadows. As the first dived down at us, I alerted your father just in time and he quickly notched an arrow at it. The second evaded my sword strike and dug its sharp claws into my cheek. I hauled it off before it could rip my eyes out and squashed its slender body with my fist. We were so preoccupied with finishing the creatures off that I never saw Freya evade the Sorceress's spell until it's red light struck my left leg. I went down instantly, my leg blazing with a hot pain. If you have ever wondered why I walk with a limp, Leonhard, well now you know."

"I could only watch as the Sorceress launched another attack at Freya, which she managed to counter. The two flashes of brilliant light found each other in the centre of the cave, sparking and crackling as they attempted to outdo each other. Then, Freya summoned all of the power she had obtained from the four crystals and began to overpower the Sorceress. As a last throw of the dice, Leona possessed your father's body, hoping her brother would protect her. It might have worked too if I hadn't dragged myself up and yanked him back. Such was the look of vexation on his face, I thought he meant to kill me for intervening. He only returned to his senses when I heard that same awful scream you and me heard in Sleima. The spell sent Leona's body flying across the cave into the healing pool, where we all watched her body sink into its depths."

With a heavy sigh, General Martine pulled himself up from his chair and started up towards his living quarters. At the top of the balcony, he took out a handkerchief from his left jacket pocket where he pressed it against his watering eyes. At once, Leonhard realised how hard it must have been for the General to talk about his past. He had clearly devoted his life to Freya's memory. At first, Leonhard wondered if Martine had stretched the fabric of truth in parts, especially when it came to the subject of the elemental crystals. Yet, seeing how upset the General was now, he now started to believe the tale.

A minute or so later, Martine returned to his office to find Leonhard studying Freya's picture.

"Her parents gave that to me when I informed them she had passed on," he said. "You see, I found Freya standing at the edge of the pool, as if she was expecting the Sorceress to rise again. As I took her in my arms, I will never forget the look on her face. It was one of peace. It reminded me of how she looked when she was younger. It was as she said her last words to me that I noticed specks of dust floating off her body. Freya's skin had turned transparent, with her arms the first part of her to disappear. And she was gone, the final specks of her twinkling above us like a star in the night sky."

The only sound that could be heard in the office was the ticking of the square table clock on Martine's desk. Leonhard waited to see if the General had any more to say and offered his condolences. He scratched the back of his head, as he was prone to do when feeling awkward.

"I had no idea about any of this."

Martine walked around to Leonhard's side and placed a warm hand on his shoulder.

"You're a good lad," he replied. "Sometimes, I wonder if Freya had actually been alive during our journey, or if she was some sort of spirit being summoned to eradicate the evil. I would like to think she was real. Even though it was only a matter of days, I really loved the time I spent with her."

"How many others know about the Sorceress, sir?"

"Only those that were alive at the time. The Continental Congress quickly decided to wipe the very memory of the Sorceress from history, seemingly worried that future generations might try and study her magic and use it to break the peace. Telling you that now, it must sound crazy."

"No, I think I can understand where they were coming from," Leonhard said. "The only thing I'm unsure of is Rufus, sir. You said you and my father saw his dead body. How can he now be alive again?"

"I wish I knew. The thing I do know is when we left the cave, his body was gone. All that remained was a pool of dried blood from where he had fallen. Somehow, in between us leaving and the Sleima mission, he had brought the Sorceress back to life."

"And the Sorceress? Now she is alive again, what do you think it is that she wants?"

Martine leant forward, his voice grave. "At this moment in time, her only ambition is to stay alive. If she regains her strength, then who knows? If there is one thing that history has taught me, it is that the lines between good and evil are often blurred. But every now and then, a person is born into this world that is destined to cause chaos. Their main ambition is only to see the world burn in the worst way possible. This is what I think of when I think of your Auntie."

"Please don't call her that," Leonhard whispered.

"Fair enough. But there will come a day when you must face up to the fact that she is of your blood."

'Maybe, but the news is still fresh. I'm not ready to accept it just yet.'

Instead, Leonhard changed the subject. "What do we do now then, sir?"

"We need to find where your father has gone and warn Luthai about the Sorceress's return. A journey to Ilsthyr would be a good place to start. We leave as soon as possible."

"You mean today?" Having just been discharged from the infirmary this morning, Leonhard was surprised to be back in the field so soon.

"Time is short," said Martine. "The plans are already in place. Vice-General Van Zandt will lead the academy in my absence and I have asked her to meet the Mayor to prepare the town's defences in case of an attack. I don't know how long we will be gone for, so do what you need to do. Meet me at the front entrance in an hour."

Stepping into the lift, Leonhard started to yawn. Listening to Martine's story had made his mind restless and his body lethargic. The lift quickly plunged to the floor below, where two students waited to board. The gate swung open and to Leonhard's surprise, Finn and Ella stepped in. Their smiles instantly warmed his heart.

"You weren't planning to leave without us, were you?" Finn asked, pressing the button for the ground floor.

"How do you know?"

"The General told us the plan first thing this morning," Ella added. "The three of us are in this together, in case you hadn't realised."

"Are you sure? I mean, we might not be back here for a while."

"We're both sure. And on the way, you can tell us what happened in Sleima."

With Ella turning towards the girls dormitories, Leonhard and Finn walked through their empty common room and opened their bedroom door. Leonhard was surprised to see his friend already packed, with his khaki green rucksack bulging at the seams. Finn took one look at Leonhard's elevated eyebrows and immediately understood, tipping his bag upside down.

"Fine, have it your way." He reached forward and shook Leonhard's hand firmly. "It is really good to have you back, man."

Leonhard could still smell Ella's sweet fragrance in his nostrils. Being back in his room with his best friend made him feel normal again.

"Thanks, Finn," he replied. "It's good to be back. I think"

Ten

The Focean army left the smouldering ruins of Sleima on the third day. The battle had been an easy test for Rufus Salt's new army, with Geralde Basquet's Nulrassan force not offering anything in the way of a resistance. The Foceans had sustained only a handful of losses and they had all been teenage boys who had been too impatient to follow Salt's strict instructions.

Knowing the city was lost, Mayor Basquet had surrendered. He reluctantly gave the captain the set of keys to gain access to the castle's vast archive room. Once inside the vault, Salt mercilessly had the Mayor executed along with the other prisoners who had surrendered.

The soldiers had gone through the dusty resources with a fine tooth comb, eventually finding what Rufus Salt had been looking for. Ancient maps, vellum bound hard books and papyrus scrolls had given him important clues to the whereabouts of the four elemental crystals. Once, he would have put them down to a figment of fantasy. Now, he had all the proof he needed they actually existed.

Before the invasion, Salt already knew the location of the Earth Crystal. Plans were already in place to steal the magical crystal and have it transported to Norr on the Sorceress's orders. He had no idea what kind of magic she could draw from them, but did know it wasn't his place to question the Sorceress.

'First of all, we must retrieve more of the Solveig blood to strengthen her,' he thought.

Much to his irritation, the young elf and his father had escaped him for now, but they both couldn't run forever. He had spent enough time in his younger days with Francis Martine to know how his mind worked.

'They are walking straight into the lion's den.'

As dawn broke, he saddled and mounted his chestnut coloured mare in one swift movement. She was a fine thing, with a smooth coat and muscular hind legs. The horse was also fast, which would be important for the journey ahead. Salt watched attentively as half of his five thousand strong army marched south. Part of him wanted to call them all back. It seemed an awful waste to part with so many men after years building up his force. Still, Terra was a huge continent. Retrieving the other crystals would take twice as long if all of his army marched in the same direction.

He had given the command of the southern army to Charles Burghwallis, a man who had provided him with a large bulk of soldiers. He trusted Burghwallis no more than any of his other Generals, but having him in temporary charge would be the only way to keep the man happy. As the last of the men faded from view, he ordered the rest of his force to pack up and prepare for the expedition north.

Whilst Salamander had been saved from certain death, the Captain had still kept him as his prisoner. He had slept little, due to hordes of soldiers noisily equipping themselves with armour and weapons in the courtyard outside his window. He knew they were getting ready to move out.

Two guards came for him at daybreak. Whilst one disposed of his heavy leg cuffs, another slid a bowl of grey gruel towards him and demanded he eat it.

Starving, Salamander did as he was told.

"Where are we going?" he asked between mouthfuls.

"North," the first guard said plainly.

"The North is a big area. Could you be any more specific?"

The second guard, a huge bald oaf, sniggered. As he did, he wiped messily at the snot streaming from his nose.

"The cap'n said it would be a surprise for you."

'I can hardly wait,' Salamander thought miserably.

He had just raised a last spoonful of the tasteless gruel to his mouth when a horn blared from the castle courtyard. At once, the two guards yanked him out of the chair and led him away from the cell.

Unlike the majority of the army on horseback, Salamander was told by one of the army Generals that he would have to walk the distance with the stable boys, cooks and camp followers.

"You cannot be serious, surely?" Salamander said back in disbelief. "Do you know who I am?"

Much like Captain Salt, the moustached General showed little emotion in his voice. He took one giant stride forward and threw Salamander head first into a pile of steaming horse muck. A ripple of laughter circled around the yard.

"Whoever you were before, you are nobody now," he said, riding off towards the front of the trail.

With his pride dented, Salamander meekly pulled himself out of the dirt, ripping the soiled jacket from his body. He had just enough time to soak his head in a pigsty before a soldier tugged at his arm chains, ordering him to start walking. The feeling that Salamander had made a grave mistake coming to Sleima grew stronger with every passing day.

The autumn morning was beautifully warm. The sun shone through the vibrant gold and crimson coloured leaves in the castle gardens, drying the ground from last night's heavy rain. The army followed a twisty mountain passageway that eventually led to the Western Terra Highway. The four lane tarmac road spanned a large part of the continent, winding through the Sandista desert in the south, passing the capital city of Akira, venturing past rolling hills and ending at the gates of Jarlstadt in Norr. A group of Focean soldiers had rode ahead and closed a large proportion of the highway to motor vehicles, meaning their initial progress would be relatively easy.

Four soldiers carried the Sorceress in a florally decorated litter. Regarding the carriage with mild amusement, Salamander attempted to work his way to the front of the crowd, planning to argue his mistreatment with Captain Salt. He felt a sharp tug on his arm chains and the oafish guard from before let him go no further. Speaking to Salt would have to wait.

As the highway bore east, the army started down a gravel path which led to a large homestead. The farmhouse itself was only a small wooden shack with a porch, but was surrounded by acres of golden barley fields. A series of brick outbuildings were located a short distance from the house, alive with the sound of livestock. Spotting the large number of mounted soldiers at his gates, a grizzled old farm owner struggled up off his rocking chair and slowly made his way down the steps to meet the Captain. His red checkered shirt failed to hide a stomach the size of a beer barrel that looked fit to burst at any moment.

"You're trespassin' on my land," the farmer shouted defiantly. "You're the one in charge, I take it?"

Salt confidently climbed off his horse and offered his hand. "I'm Captain Rufus Salt of the Focean army. Pleased to meet you."

The rosy cheeked farmer spat a stream of black fluid at Salt's feet. "Foceans up to no good as per usual! Aye, I read in the newspaper what you boys did to Sleima. Burnt it to the ground, I 'eard." He pointed a sharp looking pitchfork at Salt's midriff. "Well I won't let you do the same to my farm, you 'ear me?"

"I have no intention," Salt said, remaining cool. "All we want is a little food for the journey north. You have an abundance of cattle, I hear? My men need to keep their strength up. How about we do a trade?"

The old man mistrustingly squinted his eyes. "What do I get in return?"

"You get to keep your life. You can't say fairer than that."

It took all of three seconds for the farmer to make up his mind. "You cheeky get, ridin up 'ere like your God's gift! I'm giving you to the count of ten to get off my land. I'll call and get me boys on you, I will!"

Salt turned away and reached for the holster in his horse's saddle. At the sight of the rifle being pointed squarely at his head, the farmer promptly dropped his pitchfork and held his trembling hands high in the air.

"Please, sir. I don't want no trouble."

"Neither do I." Salt placed a hole in the centre of the farmer's head and ordered his men to search the house. They found the farmer's wife hiding under a stubby looking kitchen table and brought her outside, kicking and screaming. She died the same way as her husband. The army then went to work on slaughtering the cattle, piling the dead cow and pig carcasses in the yard.

The high pitched squeals and the sight of so many dead farm animals made Salamander squeamish. Finding him crouched down in a corner, the moustached general ordered Salamander to help the cooks prepare the meat for the hungry soldiers. As he spoke, his breath reeked of tobacco.

"You are joking, aren't you?" Salamander protested. "I've never cooked in my life."

The General took no notice and unlocked Salamander's handcuffs. He pointed at a small, dumpy woman who had started stripping the skin off a cow carcass.

"Big Bertha will look after you. She's a fine cook. Do what she says and you might get to eat a little of the meat yourself."

'Gee, aren't I lucky.'

Having no choice in the matter, Salamander walked over to the cooking area and introduced himself to the woman.

Bertha ordered Salamander to chop the beef and pork into fine pieces. He then placed them into a large cooking stove over a fire, ready to be mixed in the stew. Two young girls also helped them with the food preparation. Both sniggered every time Salamander walked past and regarded him with shy, embarrassed glances.

"Don't mind them, sonny," Bertha said to Salamander, noticing him looking in the girls direction. "They're my daughters."

"What a nice pair you have," he mocked.

"I have three more at home too. They're all by different fathers, of course." Bertha then gestured towards the girl with blonde pigtails that was stirring the stew. Salamander guessed she couldn't be more than fourteen.

"That's Annie, my eldest. She likes you, I can tell." The woman wrinkled her nose and placed a chubby hand on Salamander's shoulder. "A word of advice though, sonny. Washing yourself once in a while will go a long way."

Salamander sniffed his clothes. The smell of horse manure remained as pungent as ever on him. He intended to defend himself, but saw Bertha waddle over and try the stew with a hefty wooden spoon. By the look of satisfaction on her face, the food was ready to be served.

As Bertha and her two daughters fed and entertained the soldiers, Salamander plated up four dishes of stew and trudged over to a lofty command tent that had been erected in the centre of the farmyard. Salt had ordered his Generals in there for a meeting and wanted their food brought to them as soon as it was ready. A bushy eyebrowed soldier at the tent entrance acknowledged Salamander with a harsh sneer and lifted the flap open.

Inside, the tent was dark, save for a lantern on a compact oval bench. Salamander could hear the feeble breaths of the Sorceress inside her litter, which had been rested in the corner. The four men were huddled around the light, studying an old map.

"It is clear to me that the dwarves will make a stand at the entrance to Kahr Dovidor in the Morodir mountains," a grey haired General spoke, positioning his finger at the top of the map. "If the documents you retrieved are correct Captain, the Fire Cavern is located through these networks of tunnels. We should find the Fire Crystal there if..."

The man saw the other three looking behind him and paused. Noticing Salamander standing idly, he hastily rolled up the scroll and placed it at his side. "Are you going to serve us the food or just stand there gawping at us?"

Salamander did as he was asked, placing a plate of food in front of each of the men, as well as some chunky bread to mop it up with.

"Where are your manners, Felix?" Rufus Salt spoke. "I don't believe you've met our newest recruit. Allow me to introduce you all to Salamander Rourke, formerly of the Northwood Academy."

"He smells like horse manure."

"Ha, that would be my doing," the moustached General admitted. "I've found him to be quite disrespectful."

Salamander ignored the subsequent laughter the best he could.

"Captain Salt," he said. "May I have a word?"

"Can you not see the captain is eating, boy?" the General known as Felix said, striking Salamander with a painful elbow to his crotch. "He will speak to you later if he feels like it."

"It's quite alright," said the Captain. "I'm not that hungry anyway. Please excuse us."

Placing the black veil over his head once more, Salt followed a winded Salamander out into the yard, dismissing the guard posted at the entrance. "Anything the matter?"

Where do I start?' Salamander thought, cupping his sore crotch. He was eager to know something first.

"Where are you taking the Sorceress?"

"Horatio Godeburg has allowed us to use his academy as a base," Rufus said. "He had sent some of his students to help in Sleima, but evidently they weren't needed. It will be a safe place for the Sorceress until she grows stronger." He then crossed his arms. "But come now, I can see it in your eyes that you wanted to talk to me about something else. Army life not agreeing with you?"

"The main issue, Rufus is..."

Salt wagged his middle finger at Salamander. "Captain."

"What?"

"It is Captain Salt, to you."

Fine, have it your way if it makes you feel better.'

"The main issue, 'Captain', is that when we met in Northwood, you promised me a place in your army."

Salt shrugged. "And here you are. What is the issue?"

"I haven't been treated fairly. I hardly call cooking with that fat wench over there a good use of my abilities."

"Young man, take a look around. Every one of these soldiers have proven themselves to me or my Generals that they have what it takes to serve in the Focean army." He leaned in so close that Salamander could smell the man's acrid breath. "I had high hopes for you, to be sure. But so far, you have only proved yourself to be a failure."

In his acidic temper, Salamander reached and gripped Salt's bony arm. He noticed the man's skin was paper thin, marked and stretched. "But I'm better than any one of them!" he pleaded.

Captain Rufus stood as still as a statue, looking completely nonplussed. "Is that right? Ser Andrew! Come Here!"

A broad shouldered mountain of a man had just finished arm wrestling with a group of fellow soldiers and strode over to Salt. He towered over the pair, blocking out the sun as he saluted. "You called, Captain?"

"Salamander, I'd like you to meet Ser Andrew Merryfield. He is widely recognised as my strongest soldier." He spun towards the shaven haired brute. "Salamander has offered to challenge you to a fight. Do you accept?"

Ser Andrew answered with a sardonic grin and flexed out his huge arm muscles.

"Now wait a goddamn minute, Captain," Salamander said apprehensively. As he backed away, his t-shirt became sodden with sweat. "I didn't say anything about a fight."

"But Salamander, I don't understand. You said you were better than any one of my soldiers, did you not?. Now it is time to prove it."

A crowd of soldiers galloped over to where the brawl was about to take place, all cheering Ser Andrew on. Salt had given Salamander little choice but to fight the man. Ser Andrew had at least stripped himself of his armour at least, evening the fight a little.

Plucking up his courage, Salamander lunged forward and wrapped his arms around the wide girth of the man's waist. He attempted to push Ser Andrew to the ground but, unsurprisingly, he was unmoved. It was like trying to move a heavy boulder. The reply was a heavy blow to Salamander's skull that sent him spinning to the ground, followed by a kick to the chest.

Ser Andrew seemed to be lapping up the applause of his comrades, parading himself around Salamander's crumpled body. Salt watched on with interest, arms crossed at all times. Salamander avoided the next kick by rolling his body to the right and, somehow, staggered back to his feet. He brushed the mud away from his face and beckoned for the soldier to charge.

"Over here, you dumb barbarian!"

Ser Andrew swept towards him, but Salamander ducked at the last moment and leapt to safety. The man looked perplexed as he attempted to strike again, only for Salamander to pull the same move again. "Hold still, will you?"

It appeared that Salamander's evasive strategy was working. He had quickly acknowledged that he hadn't a cat in hells chance in defeating Ser Andrew in single combat, so he needed to be clever. He would make the man work until he became too tired, and then try and strike him down.

Whilst the crowd became annoyed at Salamander's tactics, Salt watched on regardless. There was a hint of a wily smile in the mouth hole of his mask.

After fifteen minutes of running around, Ser Andrew folded his body over to catch his breath, feeling physically exhausted. Sensing the opportunity, Salamander darted forward and struck him with a fist to the side of his face. The man gripped his cheek in pain and bawled out loudly. He quickly attempted to do the same to the other side, but tripped over Ser Andrew's dangling leg and fell face first into the mud. With a heavy grunt, Ser Andrew knelt and lifted Salamander up by his t-shirt as if he was a small mouse. He was defenceless to block the rapid left hooks that landed in his face, almost relieved when he was flung to the floor.

His body aching and beaten, Salamander spat out a broken tooth and saw his opponent's ugly face staring down at him. A ringing sound in his ears blocked out all other sounds. Time seemed to slow down and almost stand still. The soldiers were cheering Ser Andrew on, buoyed by his last move. Salamander saw the soldier's huge fist slowly encroach towards his head and knew this would be the punch that finished him off. Twenty years of life would be gone in an instant, and what did he have to show for it? He would die an embarrassment and a failure.

The contours of Ser Andrew's face suddenly began to change. The look of narrowed determination remained, but the shaven head was replaced by wild ginger hair. His deep brown eyes now shone the colour of emeralds and his ears had somehow grown bigger. Ser Andrew no longer stood over him. Instead, it was Salamander's father. How was this possible?

'I killed you, you evil son of a bitch. I watched you burn as a punishment for everything you did to me.'

Was Salamander hallucinating this moment? Had his father magically returned from the dead in a horrible twist of revenge, just long enough to see his son's life expire? All of the awful memories of the physical beatings he had taken as a boy came flooding back to him.

'I won't let you win, Dad,' Salamander thought, feeling his blood boiling. *'Not this time. I won't let you win, I won't let you win, I won't...'*

Finding an unholy burst of strength, Salamander caught the approaching fist and twisted his father's arm around one hundred and eighty degrees. The next thing he knew, he was on top of his father, hitting his face like a man possessed. He was having an out of body experience, unable to control himself.

When Salamander eventually came around, he saw that his hands were bleeding profusely. He looked down at the man's face. It had now morphed itself back to Ser Andrew's, though a lot bloodier and bruised than before. The man's muscular chest rose weakly for the final time and stayed flat. The gathering crowd fell silent, trying to comprehend what had just happened.

"It seems I was wrong about you," Salt said carefully, placing a hand on Salamander's shoulder. "You will be needing a uniform and Ser Andrew's horse. Arise, Ser Salamander! We have a long journey ahead."

Eleven

The day had been a radiant blue when Leonhard left the infirmary that morning. Now, in between General Martine revealing his past to Leonhard and him collecting his things from his room, the sky had turned a threatening slate grey. Raindrops, which seemed innocuous at first, hammered down on the three mercenaries like bullets.

'Typical Northwood weather then,' he thought.

He, Finn and Ella each took shelter underneath an archway next to the front entrance to the academy, waiting for the General to arrive.

"Are you sure he said to meet here?" Finn asked, studying his watch.

"For the final time, yes!" Leonhard said.

To his left, he heard an engine backfire. Seconds later, he saw a white saloon peer over the parking lot slope and swing towards their vicinity. General Martine was driving the car, with Xai in the passenger's seat. As it pulled up to them, the three young mercenaries dived in the back and the vehicle set off towards Northwood's train station.

Sea mist overhung the fields and mountains that surrounded the academy. Gaping out of the back window, Leonhard could only make out the outline of the three stacked rings that constituted the academy's floor levels and the seven tunnels that splintered off from the central plaza. From a distance, he had always likened the building's appearance to a bloated bronze airship. He emitted a long, deep breath. The academy had been like a second home to him. He wondered when it would be when he saw it again.

"Christ!" Martine cursed, working the wheel. "I can't see a thing!" The dense afternoon mist had swallowed up Northwood's pier, meaning visibility was almost non-existent. The windscreen wipers were doing their best to clear the streams of water, but still it didn't help the General navigate the clogged roads. "What time is our train again, Xai?"

The woman looked at a piece of paper on her lap. "Two o'clock. It says we need to pick up the tickets from the booth fifteen minutes beforehand."

She scanned the busy road ahead and pointed towards a side street on the right.

"We might be better going that way, Francis."

Martine agreed and quickly turned away from the pier. In his haste, the General swerved to narrowly miss the oncoming trolley bus. Cursing under his breath, he followed the street under the base of a grey stone railway viaduct and up a steep incline. Thankfully, the traffic thereafter became considerably lighter.

"I'm glad Percy isn't coming with us this time," Finn commented. "Aren't you, guys?"

Both Leonhard and Ella ignored him. The issue he had with Percy was his and his alone.

Instead, Ella wiped the condensation from the side window and looked out. The Mayor's house had been built on the highest part of the town and could usually be seen for miles around. Today though, the mist had made her parents' place practically invisible. She knew she should have visited her father before he left, but she hadn't felt like seeing him after the Sleima mission. Ella promised herself that she would drop in on their return, mainly to see her mother, who she cared for deeply.

Martine pulled up outside the train station with ten minutes to spare. Xai swiftly ran inside to pick up their tickets. The academy field operative had to fight her way through the other passengers that had gathered on the steps, trying to take shelter from the torrent of water above. Martine pulled on his top hat and gestured for the other mercenaries to follow him.

The station was a deluge of noise as raindrops drummed on the glass panelled roof. A smell of roasted coffee beans from the station cafe filled the air as Martine led the mercenaries past the timing boards to platform three. Standing in front of a chugging black steam train, Xai handed them each a pink ticket.

"Apparently, all trains in and out of Ilsthyr station have been cancelled until further notice," she told them, her face despondent. "I have told the conductor it is a matter of emergency. He had agreed to drop you all off at an abandoned station outside the Durgan Marshes." She then shrugged apologetically. "It's the best I could do."

Martine swallowed hard. The marshes were an inhospitable place, located on the fringes of the forest of Ilsthyr. To say it had a dark history was putting it mildly; three hundred years ago, a bloody battle between the elves of Ilsthyr and the dwarves of Kahr Dovidor had scarred the landscape, with thousands of fallen soldiers left to rot into the earth. Two centuries later, humans first inhabited the eastern side of Terra. Coal had been discovered at the fringes of the marsh and they began mining the area for the resource. A year after opening, the coal board visited the Durgan Mine to perform a routine inspection. They found the place abandoned. The hundred strong workforce had vanished, never to be heard from again.

Many travellers had crossed the mines and claimed to have seen strange sightings. Was it haunted? Of course, there would have been a time when Martine wouldn't have believed such nonsense. But the sights he had seen in his life had opened his mind to any possibility.

He knew that cutting through the marshes would be the quickest way to Ilsthyr. The next train station would be fifty miles further south at the old mining town of Los Reyes.

"It seems we will have to walk awhile to get there," Martine said to his students, folding his ticket in his jacket pocket. He acknowledged Xai and climbed onto the locomotive. "Let's go."

With several blaring whistles, the steam train pulled away from Northwood station. It slowly gathered speed along the tracks that spanned across the murky ocean. Martine led the group through the aisles of two sparsely populated carriages and opened the sliding door to a lavishly decorated private cabin. A gold plated sign on the wall told them it was *Reserved for Representatives of Northwood Military Academy.'*

"This place is like a palace!" Finn said, bouncing up and down on the plush corner settee. Four modest sized bunk beds were also provided for missions that required longer travel.

"I'm glad you like it, Finn," Martine replied, slumping himself down at the far corner of the settee. "The diversion through the marshes isn't ideal, but if we set a good pace, we will reach Ilsthyr by tomorrow morning."

"I wonder why King Luthai has closed the station," Leonhard mused. The small wooden station had been built under the King's rule as he opened Ilsthyr to outside trade for the first time. Luthai was a clever man; he sensed it could benefit both elves and humans alike. Of course, many Elven traditionalists had protested against the King's request. However, it had brought a greater level of prosperity to the city. To suddenly close the gates again after so many years suggested something serious had happened in the city.

"It does strike me as an odd thing to do," Martine agreed. "Hopefully things will become clearer soon."

Finn strode across the room and slid the cabin door open. He poked his head out and scanned the aisle from left to right.

"I'm famished," he confessed. "I'm gonna see if there is a food trolley or somethin'!"

"We both ate this morning!" Ella reminded him. "Is food all you ever think about?"

He replied with a cheeky wink. "I would say it's definitely in the top three, along with Hardball and women."

"Tch, tch! I don't know how he keeps a slim figure with the amount that he eats."

If truth be told, Ella was a little jealous of Finn. Like when her mother had been when she had been younger, it was a daily battle for Ella to keep the weight off her figure.

'Not now though, mother. You have no worries about that now...'

The train made its first stop at the port town of Tulusa and then wound its way through the landscape. A tinny sounding announcement on the intercom system told the group that their requested stop was next. Leonhard paid a visit to the bathroom and met the others at the exit doors. As the train slowed to a halt, what he then saw out of the misty windows shocked him. The abandoned platform at the Durgan Marshes looked rather forlorn, with moss and weeds sprouting through the crumbling concrete. The walls of the brick and limestone central terminal were scarred with graffiti. It had a spooky feel to it, as light filtered through one end of the windows to the other.

As soon as the mercenaries stepped onto the dilapidated platform, the train's wheels began turning again. It seemed to Leonhard that even the train conductor was afraid of the unnerving chill in the air. The way that the mist muffled the sound of the moving locomotive turned his spine cold.

"Geez, this place is a dump," Finn said. He stubbed the edge of the platform with his heel, sending shards of concrete plummeting onto the tracks. "We must be the first passengers here for..."

"...nearly thirty years," Martine finished. He glanced up at the terminal building nervously. "Come on. It is wise that we don't linger here any longer than we have to."

Crossing over the train tracks, the group found a gap through a large ivy covered wire fence. The steel winding towers of the underground mine shaft loomed large above them, rising high in an imposing manner. The columns had turned orange with rust and one of the stairwells that led to the top had collapsed in on itself.

Even without knowing it's history, Leonhard could feel it in his blood that something catastrophic had happened here. His senses had been pricked by the wind that hurled around them, sounding as if a gathering of lost souls were crying out in pain. Yet, the branches of the trees in the distance never moved. There was also a complete absence of any birdsong. A fear ran through him so immediate and so sharp that it felt as if a thousand insects were crawling on his skin.

"Let's keep going," he urged towards the group.

"You feel it too?" Ella whispered, similarly spooked.

Leonhard nodded. For once, he was glad it wasn't just him.

The mist grew even thicker as they proceeded deeper into the marsh, with the winding path in front increasingly harder to follow. Finn donned his navy Northwood jacket again, feeling the damp air creep onto his bare neck and arms. He almost lost his footing on one particular occasion as the boggy ground narrowed.

He peered down at the greenish coloured water. A body, possibly a fallen soldier lay on his back in the shallow depths of the marsh, staring lifelessly at the heavens.. His tall height and pointed ears signified he was of an elven heritage.

"Have you seen...?"

Finn didn't finish the last word, noticing General Martine and Ella were following the path someway in front. He moved further towards the surface of the water, arching his neck over for a better look. Only now, the bog was littered with bodies as far as his eyes could see! Finn rubbed at his eye sockets, just to make sure he wasn't seeing things.

There had only been one dead elf in the water a moment ago. Now there were twenty, maybe thirty.

What was going on?

Eager to know he wasn't just seeing things, Finn slowly drew his hand into the water. He reached further, his fingers touching the dead elf's face. Instantly, he felt a deep sense of revulsion. The surface of the skin felt completely wrong. It was soft and slimy, comparable to touching the body of a slippery eel. He tried to pull back, but his arm seemingly wanted to explore further. Unseen by Finn, the elf had moved his head and was no longer peering at the sky.

It was staring directly at him, with his razor sharp teeth bared in a menacing grin.

Finn could feel himself being pulled under, his arms thrashing about uselessly. He wasn't strong enough to fight back. His face crashed into the water. For a brief moment, he saw the hideous creatures that lay waiting for him underneath, dragging him under the depths of the marsh with their skin piercing claws, intent on ripping him to pieces.

"Finn! What are you doing?" Martine waded in the water and yanked the young man's shoulders.

Finn shot out a stream of water and sat back, breathless. "They were pulling me in, sir!" he cried. "Look at them all!"

Disbelief spread across the General's face as he leaned over the side of the bank. "I don't see anything, Finn. All I saw was you falling in."

"But, but surely..."

He pulled himself up and looked over. The General was right. The lake was empty. There was nothing to see but the murky green water.

No fallen elven soldiers lying on the sea bed.

No monsters lurking under the surface.

Had he somehow imagined the whole thing?

"It doesn't matter," Finn said eventually, wiping his glasses clean of the gunk.

"This damn marsh can play tricks on you. Keep your wits about you and don't believe everything you see." Martine then looked around in a panic. "Where is Leonhard?"

"He's not with you, sir?"

Martine shouted Leonhard's name out loud. Ella emerged through the reeds and did the same. There was no answer. The marsh had grown deadly quiet. "Come on, both of you," Martine ordered. "We need to find him quickly!"

As Finn started back again, he winced as he felt a sharp pain in his right arm. Rolling his wet sleeve up, he noticed four little marks just below his wrist.

Four marks that looked suspiciously like the marks a sharp claw would have made.

Leonhard was a distance behind the rest of the group. He had not moved in over a minute. His attention had been directed towards a ruined archway of dark stone, which he figured was a remnant of an ancient monastery. A heavily armoured man, no more than four feet in height, stood in the middle of the archway. His small eyes regarded Leonhard vacantly and he sniffed the air with his hooked nose. His deep red beard protruded all the way down to his feet. Leonhard recognised the man to be a dwarf from the Morodir Mountains to the north. The question was why was he here, in the middle of the marsh?

As Leonhard moved nearer, the dwarf scuttled under the archway and faded into the mist. Leonhard knew he should warn the others, but his raised voice might scare the dwarf off even more.

'He might be lost,' he thought innocently. Giving into his inhibitions, Leonhard followed.

Moss covered rubble littered the pathway. As he climbed over one particular large boulder, he caught sight of the dwarf climbing a stone stairwell into a ruined cloister.

Leonhard felt the air press close around him. The darkening shadows sharpened his vision. He knew the safest thing would be to turn back, as General Martine and the others would surely now be looking for him. He stood at the foot of the stairs in a quandary.

'What harm would it do just to look?' he thought to himself.

'There might be something bad up there,' a second inner voice warned.

'So? I have my bow and arrows with me. If father were in my shoes, he would do the same.'

'Don't bring up my father! He's the reason why I'm here!"

He swung his foot onto the first step, eager to quieten the two battling voices inside his head.

Reaching the top, Leonhard gasped and steadied himself, not quite believing what he was seeing. A large silver birch tree had sprouted through the broken floor, covering what was once an altar. The dwarf was nowhere to be seen. Instead, a dozen sizeable bird eggs were nestled high on a stone dais in the centre of the ruined room. Intrigued, Leonhard stroked his hand across the waxy red substance of the largest one, noticing the strange ripples and craters that formed on its surface. Gripping it in both hands, he was surprised to find how heavy the egg was.

A sense of wonder quickly turned to trepidation as the egg began to beat furiously. The host inside kicked and screamed, eager to be free. He quickly placed it back on the dais as a crack formed at the top, rapidly working its way down the surface of the egg. Steam erupted from its pores and as the egg broke into two pieces, hot orange liquid shot out in multiple directions. Leonhard felt it land on his jacket and solidify instantly.

The creature inside was dead, twisted in body and ugly in appearance. It's wide eyes stared accusingly at Leonhard. It looked nothing like he had seen before.

'I really must show the others this.'

Turning back towards the stairwell, Leonhard caught a shadow move swiftly out of the corner of his eye. He glanced upwards just in time to spot an enormous bird swoop down at him, moving with intent. He leapt to his left and narrowly avoided it's outstretched talons. The bird squawked at him with its bright yellow beak, causing the ground beneath to shake.

Adrenaline took over as Leonhard quickly fired an arrow, which deflected off the feathered beast's scaly wing and out of sight. Cursing, he hid behind the dais, giving himself a moment's respite. Blood pounded in his ears and his heart was stuck in his throat. He exhaled a deep breath and pushed himself up once more, loading another arrow as he moved.

Inches away from his face, Leonhard scanned the whole of the bird for the first time. It's deep black eyes contradicted the bright red colour of its face and yellow beak. It's rear was even more unusual; the muscular body and hind legs resembled an animal such as a large cat.

'Heavens above, it's a Griffin!' he realised. 'What is it doing this far south?'

The mythical creatures usually resided in the cool north, sometimes as far as the Ice Continent. Leonhard had never seen a griffin up this close before. Famed for its incredible power, the griffin was a beautiful creature, yet hideous at the same time. He was under no illusion that he would pay the ultimate price for murdering the griffin's baby.

There was only one thing for it; to strike first. At this distance, there was no need to fire another arrow. Leonhard vaulted forward and impaled the arrowhead in the beast's right eye, driving it in through the soft flesh and gristle with all of his might. The griffin stumbled backwards and cried out with a piercing shriek, flapping his wings rapidly.

Sensing his time to escape, Leonhard sprinted down the stone stairwell. Three quarters of the way down, he heard a scuffled movement behind him. He turned his head to see if he was being followed and foolishly missed the next step, collapsing at the bottom in a heap.

His arrows fell from his quiver and scattered in all directions. The wind had been knocked out of Leonhard's lungs and a trickle of blood ran from his nose. With a grunt, he forced himself up into a sitting position. The griffin perched on the top step of the cloister, it's vexed face screaming murder. Blind in one eye, it waited attentively for Leonard's next move.

He counted to three and darted towards the archway. Just as the ruin came into view, he heard the griffin make a dive for him. Leonhard ducked his head at the last possible moment and threw himself forward. The beast let out a cry of frustration and landed hard on top of the archway, causing several pieces to splinter off.

His escape was blocked.

Leonhard had nowhere to go.

The creature took off again, aiming lower this time. It covered the distance swiftly and dug its claws sharply into the elf's chest.

A torrent of pain spiralled through him as he was forced to the floor. Leonhard reached for a stray arrow. Frustratingly, it was too far away.

He looked upwards at the griffin's open beak. His vision became blocked with the pink flesh of its mouth. As it moved in for the kill, Leonhard reached with both hands towards the hard muscle of its pink tongue and squeezed vigorously.

Caught in a moment of surprise and agony, the griffin never heard the approaching reinforcements. Ella threw her sword desperately at its neck, stunning the beast instantly as the pointy end emerged through the other side.

Finn managed to pull Leonhard clear as General Martine climbed on the griffin's scaly back. He swung his broadsword and severed its head with one mighty stroke. The creature gave one last defeated roar of fury and crashed lifelessly to the ground.

"Are you hurt?" Martine shouted, holding his hands on Leonhard's cheeks.

Leonhard stared back blankly, lost for words at what had just happened.

'If they had arrived just ten seconds later...'

"Leonhard, answer me! Are you hurt?"

He shook his head in reply. The griffin's head lay at his side in a pool of orange blood. It's body gave one final spasm and lay still.

Leonhard's legs quickly gave way at the sight of the dead beast. He felt the contents of his stomach rise up his gullet and vomited.

"What possessed you to follow this path?" Martine persisted, anger present in his voice. "You could have been killed!"

Finn and Ella helped Leonhard get back to his feet.

"I...I saw something," he replied, throat burning from the bile.

"I knew it was a mistake cutting through the marshes!" Martine looked in anguish at the sky. "We are starting to lose the light. It is imperative that we get to the other side before nightfall. We must hurry!"

The General led the group back onto the main path. He informed Leonhard that he and Ella had found a route through the marsh, only to have been forced back when he realised both Leonhard and Finn were missing.

As they moved ahead into the heart of the marsh, the reed bed grew thicker and higher. In no time at all, the stems towered above the party, the light all but dissipating. Martine persevered, cutting straight through the bed, despite the path becoming almost non-existent. The group had no choice but to trust him and follow.

Leonhard grew frustrated as the minutes wore on. He felt the long strands cutting his outstretched arms, with one in particular drawing a trickle of blood. His skin had grown cold to the touch, yet covered with droplets of sweat. The way the reeds pressed in on him made him feel incredibly claustrophobic. Both his chest and back ached from the battle with the griffin.

Just when he thought this hell would never end, the group found a gap leading to a riverbank. Leonhard noticed that the mist had started to recede, making the air feel somewhat cleaner. On the horizon, a hazy sunshine started to retreat behind a forest in the distance.

'Ilsthyr!' he realised. *'We have nearly made it.'*

To reach the forest before sundown, the mercenaries would have to negotiate an archipelago. Each member made easy work of the first three islets and a large log made a natural bridge to the fourth.

General Martine, Leonhard and Ella made it across without incident. Unsure of himself, Finn decided to scan further upstream for another way across.

"What are you waiting for?" Martine called to him, impatiently.

"I might fall in, sir."

"We haven't got time for this, Finn. Come on!"

Out of options, Finn closed his eyes and mentally prepared himself for the crossing. He let go of his negative thoughts and started across. His right foot soon became tangled in some algae at the edge of the riverbank and he hit the water face first.

Howls of laughter then emerged from Ella and Leonhard as he sheepishly swam towards them. Even Martine allowed himself a small chuckle.

'It feels good to laugh again,' Leonhard thought, helping his friend out of the water.

"I told you'd I fall in," Finn said, wiping seaweed off his face. "I always make a fool of myself."

The group arrived at the outer reaches of the Elven forest just as dusk approached. To stop Finn catching a chill, Martine handed the mercenary a spare set of clothes from his rucksack.

"They're slightly big, sir," Finn remarked, pulling on the ill fitted trousers and oversized jacket.

Martine seemed unconcerned.

"They will do until your old ones dry," he said.

He told Finn and Ella to prepare the food from their rations, whilst he and Leonhard went into the forest to gather wood for the fire.

The darkness in the forest smelled humid, with the air silent and still. The trees on the outer ridges consisted of ancient oaks and newer, but no less inspiring elms. Taking in the sight of the woodland, it came to Leonhard how much he had missed home.

He found a pile of gnarly branches on the forest floor not too far from the camp and started to strip the bark off the wood. Martine climbed onto a thick fallen log and whacked a thick branch above his head with his sword. It broke off from the main tree trunk and crashed into the soft ground.

"I'm sorry if I was slightly hard on you back there, Leonhard," Martine said, now that they were alone. He studied the elf. "Is something on your mind?"

"What do you mean?"

"You have that troubled look on your face. I could always tell when your father was bothered by something."

Leonhard had been unsure whether to tell the General about his previous night's dream of the Sorceress. The meaning of the dream had played on his mind all day, suffocating his thoughts. He was, in truth, eager to gather Martine's opinion on it.

"Do you think it was a coincidence that I dreamed of her?" Leonhard asked afterwards. "It seemed so real! For a short time, I was Leona."

Martine froze. A ripple of panicked dread worked its way through his ageing figure. Possessing another person's body was a highly specialised and dangerous type of magic, even in a dream like state. Martine had no illusions how serious this was.

'I know what this means and I should tell him, but it would only worry him further. The lad is in a fragile state as it is. He has had a lot to contend with over the past few days. One step at a time...'

Instead, Martine climbed down and ruffled the elf's blonde locks. "I'm sure it means nothing." He had aimed to reassure Leonhard without sounding too fake. "Like you said, it was only a dream."

Leonhard frowned, straightening his hair back. He wondered why the General was acting so strange. "Well, if you say so..."

"I do!" Martine eagerly changed the subject. "Let's head back to camp and see how they're getting on. I'm famished."

As they both carried the firewood they had collected, Martine wondered if he would later regret not telling Leonhard the importance of the dream and what it meant for his future. He ultimately decided to tell Leonhard's father first once they had found him and take it from there.

Once the fire had been built and lit, Finn and Ella placed the chopped potatoes and carrots in a pot to boil. Ella had also found some dried chicken in the rations to go with the vegetables. It was a plain meal and could have done with some sauce, but after the day they all had, no one was complaining. Each of their stomachs were rumbling loudly by the time it came to serve the food and it was devoured quickly.

"So Leonhard, is this Luther guy as fat as everybody describes him?" Finn asked, spitting pieces of chicken in all directions.

"It's Luthai, but that's okay," Leonhard said, smiling. "King Luthai Hassein, the twelfth of his family to rule Ilsthyr. And yes, he is rather large!"

Martine chuckled. "That's putting it mildly, I think," he said, stabbing a piece of potato with his fork. "The only time I have ever seen Luthai not eating is to fill up his wine glass." He held a brief pause. "His heart is in the right place though. The King will help us, I'm sure of it."

"I sure hope you are right, sir," Leonhard replied glumly.

When the food was finished, Martine tied a piece of tarpaulin to two of the trees, shielding the camp in case any rain fell during the night.

"I suggest we retire for the evening," he suggested. "We have a big day ahead of us tomorrow."

Leonhard nodded and started off towards the woods. Ella watched the elf until he was out of sight.

"He's gone to pray to his Gods, in case you were wonderin'," Finn said from his spot by the fire.

"Does he always do that?" Ella asked, intrigued by Leonhard's actions.

Finn prodded the weakening flames with a large stick, causing the embers to spark into life once more.

"Aye, every night. There's no point disturbin' him when he's on his knees."

'I still have so much to learn about him,' Ella thought. Finn had told her that Leonhard was a complex being at the best of times. With everything that had happened to him in the last few days, she knew the elf must be hurting and confused inside.

'When he's ready to talk, I can be there for him. We just need some time alone, away from everything else that is going on.'

The sky overhead was dark, the stars bright and plentiful. She noticed the moon had returned to its normal colour after the previous night's phenomenon. Finn left her alone by the fire and crawled into his sleeping bag, snoring as soon as his head hit the pillow. With a last longing look towards the bushes, Ella pulled the covers over her and shut her eyes.

A hand on the shoulder roused her from a deep sleep. She brushed it off, mumbling softly and turned the other way.

"Ella, wake up!"

She rubbed her eyes and opened them slowly, noticing that it was still dark. The fire had burned down to smoky cinders, flickering only an occasional spark. General Martine and Finn were already awake, weapons in their hands. Leonhard leant over her, looking panicked.

"What's wrong?" she asked him, groggily.

"There's someone coming," he whispered back. He gestured towards the clearing he had returned from only a couple of hours ago. "They're coming from in there!"

Ella threw the covers off her and joined the others at the edge of the forest, listening with slight trepidation at the approaching footsteps. The sound of twigs snapping reverberated around them as the intruders made their way through the undergrowth. With the unforgiving marsh to the south of their camp, there would be nowhere for the mercenaries to hide.

Twenty elven soldiers swarmed the group, each carrying a threatening silver bow. Leonhard recognised their horned helmets and orange cloaks instantly. His father had worn the same Royal Guard uniform in his younger days before his promotion to King Luthai's anointed bodyguard. Leonhard approached the guards with a contented sigh, swinging his bow back over his right shoulder.

"Leonhard, what are you doing?" Martine whispered urgently.

"It's ok, I know these men," he replied, gesturing for his party to drop their weapons.

Or at least he thought he knew them. A soldier, towering in height stepped towards him and took off the horned helmet. Leonhard assumed the soldier to be the male squadron leader. Instead, it was a blonde haired woman, her face aggressive and unfamiliar.

"State your mission!" she urged at once in a broken human accent.

Leonhard started to tell her when Martine cut in.

"Whatever we are doing here is our business," he said coldly. "It is of no concern to you."

The female soldier arched an eyebrow. "When you are trespassing on our land and stealing wood from the sacred forest, it is our concern." She raised her gloved hand in the air and the soldiers at her back proceeded to load their bows.

"Wait!" Leonhard shouted, eager to break the tension. "We only wish to speak to King Luthai. My name is Leonhard Solveig, son of Ruven Solveig, the King's bodyguard. The man to my right is General Francis Martine of the Northwood Academy. We only ask that you grant us safe passage through."

Leonhard had thought by revealing who they were would solve the matter. Instead, it seemed to aggravate the soldiers even further. Their weapons now pointed directly at each of their chests.

"King Luthai is dead, little elf," the woman said, her face as hard as stone. "His son, Rashmir, rules Ilsthyr now."

'Dead. No, it can't be!' Leonhard felt a sudden sinking feeling in the pit of his stomach. "How did his highness die?"

He thought it was a fair question, but it only seemed to amuse the squadron. The female elf remained expressionless throughout.

"You mean you don't know? He was killed by your father's hand. The same man who swore to protect his Highness. Your father is a traitor and a murderer! He must be brought to justice!"

Twelve

The group marched on in silence as they made their way deeper into the forest. Early morning sunlight pierced through the silhouettes of the tall pine trees as the first fingers of dawn crept into the day. A herd of deer watched the passers-by with intent, turning back to graze the nearby foliage only when the danger had passed. Closing his eyes as he marched, Leonhard found the rustling of autumn leaves in the wind and the morning chorus of birdsong above his head relaxing. It allowed his mind to momentarily waver from the horrible truth that his father had been accused of regicide. The shock of it felt as if someone had slapped him across the face. His body felt numb and his eyes burned from the tears.

'Why, father?' he kept asking himself. 'Why would you do such a thing?'

His mind flickered to the new King. Leonhard had spoken to Rashmir on numerous occasions, but wouldn't go as far as regarding him as a friend. Would they get any help from him? He doubted it.

Francis Martine hadn't believed the female soldier in the slightest. He knew Ruven Solveig well enough to know he was ultimately devoted to his King. He had been persistent in demanding more details into what happened. The woman ignored him at first and then ordered one of her soldiers to tie coarse rope around his mouth, silencing his questions.

The Elven soldiers had forced the mercenaries to climb through the undergrowth for a short time before finding a well-worn wooden boardwalk. Arrow pointed way markers situated at every mile directed the group towards the settlement. Snaking its way through the woods, the path began to widen and followed the contours of the nearby river. Finn was eager for something to drink, so cupped his hands in the flowing water. The water was slightly brown, but he had gone beyond caring.

"Get back on your feet, human!" a bulbous nosed guard shouted at him. Rather recklessly, he struck the back of Finn's head with the end of his bow. "We will tell you when to stop."

Finn turned to the soldier with his fists held out, his expression a mixture of pain and anger. "Do that again, I dare ya!"

The soldier caught the threat and moved again. The female leader blocked the soldier's bow mid-strike and stood over him.

"Did I ask you to hit the prisoner?" she asked forcefully.

Feeling humiliated, the soldier lowered his head in shame.

"No, Frau Helga," he mumbled. "I only thought..."

"You thought nothing!" she snarled back, her nostrils flaring like an angry hound. "Disobey my orders again and I will ask the rest of my team to hang you from the nearest tree. Understood?"

He eyed the woman warily. "I do. Yes, ma'am."

As she strode past Finn, he shot her a look of gratitude. Frau Helga returned it with disgust that suggested the human meant nothing to her. Finn understood then that she didn't intervene to help him, only acting to reinforce her power over the squadron. He hated her for that.

As the sun moved overhead, the forest became hot and humid. It was a complete contrast to the cool mist that plagued them yesterday through the Durgan Marshes. To reach Ilsthyr itself, the group had to step inside the trunk of a humongous fallen oak tree. Wooden niche steps had been eloquently carved in the bark, leading steeply upwards. Lit torches on each side made visibility easier. A guard patrolling the top acknowledged Frau

Helga in Elvish and signalled to the five counterparts around him to open the chain linked gate that allowed access to the city.

The elves had built the Ilsthyr settlement high above the forest floor, with their arboreal dwellings connected by a vast array of rope bridges, wooden walkways and circular platforms. Spiral staircases had been carved into the tall pine trees to allow its residents to navigate the various levels. The warm sun shone on them, drawing out all of the pine's sweet fragrance. Ella stood on the highest platform in awe, taking in the forest sprawl in front of her.

'It's more beautiful than I imagined,' she realised. The air was incredibly clean and pure, unlike Northwood, where you could taste the pollution on your tongue. Her father had spent some time in Ilstyhr when Ella was younger, meeting the King to discuss a new trade deal. He had described the city to her in avid detail during one of her bedtime stories, right down to how elves lived and communicated with each other. He had even taught her some basic words of the elven language. Whether she had been too young to comprehend it, her father's words hadn't actually done the city justice.

"Quit dawdling," a soldier demanded from her, pulling at the knots around her arms.

Ella sighed.

'They're not as welcoming as you described though, father. Especially if these soldiers are anything to go by.'

The group descended a rope bridge, leading to a tree lined marketplace. Leonhard immediately knew that something was amiss. Judging by the position of the sun, it was now mid-morning and traders would usually be setting up their stalls for a busy evening. Instead, a further group of soldiers congregated in the centre, waiting to be measured up and equipped with leather armour. A bushy bearded fletcher sat across from a stone jig, feathering arrows with rapid speed. He glanced up at the prisoners with a cautious distrust, grunting as he returned to his work.

They are preparing for battle,' Leonhard realised. *'But against which enemy?'* He asked the guard nearest to him the same question, but received no answer.

Amongst the strangers, he finally spied a familiar face performing repairs to a rope bridge. He knew the elf to be called Roderich, once Leonhard's neighbour. Although Roderich was now well advanced in years, he could often outwork many younger than him. He and his wife had often looked after a young Leonhard whilst his father was working late at the Royal Palace or had travelled away with the King. Seeing his neighbour again, still with his cropped salt and pepper goatee beard, made Leonhard's heart swell with comfort. Finally, there was someone who could talk some sense into this madness. He pulled clear of the soldier's firm grip and ran over.

"Roderich, it's so good to see you!" Leonhard spoke to him in Elvish.

Completely engrossed in his work, Roderich had failed to notice the shadow fall over him. Leonhard's greeting startled the elf, making him drop his chisel. He wiped the sweat away from his flushed forehead and shielded his eyes from the sun.

"Well I'll be damned," he replied in a curt manner. "Leonhard Solveig has returned to Ilsthyr!" He took heed of the rope tied around Leonhard's hands and spat directly into his face. "So you were involved in his highness's death too, huh?"

Leonhard felt numb with shock. He wiped the spit away with his sleeve. "What? No, Roderich you don't understand. My father..."

Roderich grew deaf to his protests. He placed his hands over Leonhard's shoulders and started shaking him vigorously, as if he were a nothing more than a baby's rattle.

"I don't want to hear any more of your lies, Leonhard! You and your father disgust me!"

Frau Helga had heard enough and ordered her soldiers to intervene. The two elves directly behind Leonhard pried Roderich away, each aiming an armoured fist squarely towards his stomach. The elderly elf fell to the ground, heaving in pain.

Despite his old neighbour's actions, Leonhard felt a trace of sympathy towards him. He wondered if every elf in Ilsthyr believed the same as old Roderich. He prayed to his gods that it wasn't the case.

The Royal Palace eventually came into view. Nestled on top of the highest point in the forest, the building looked imposing, yet inviting at the same time. Whilst most buildings in Ilsthyr had been built out of reclaimed wood, the rectangular shaped palace and the white domed Temple of Odin in its grounds were crafted from the highest quality granite. A gushing waterfall ran away from the temple, falling into the lake they had followed earlier. The soldier known as Frau Helga led her prisoners up a series of steep steps that meandered its way up the mountainside.

"Aw man, I don't suppose you Elves have ever thought about buildin' a lift?" Finn said, groaning at the climb ahead. His body ached all over from the long walk, with his leg muscles crying out for mercy. More than anything, he hated heights and saw that no guardrail had been erected to catch the unwary. His legs quickly turned to jelly.

Of course, it had been a climb that Leonhard had made hundreds of times before. As a boy, he had thought nothing of it. He always had enjoyed running up the steps and counting them out loud. He knew from memory it was four hundred and sixty seven steps to the top. Nothing could beat the feeling of climbing higher and higher until you felt as if you were flying above the trees. The view from the top was spectacular, especially during the snows of the winter months. Leonhard knew Finn well enough to know the view would be the last thing on his mind, however. "Shut your eyes and you'll make it," he advised.

"What if I fall?"

"You won't! I promise."

"If you say so." Finn looked behind him and lowered his voice to a whisper. "What kind of name is 'Frau Helga', anyway?"

"All male elf knights have the title of 'Herr' before their first name. My father is known as 'Herr Ruven.' It's the equivalent to 'Ser' for human soldiers. There are only a handful of female knights in the Elven army and they go by the title of 'Frau.'"

"She should go by the title of 'Queen Bitch' after how she has treated us!"

"Point noted," said Leonhard, smiling. "The strange thing is that I have never even seen her before. I can only guess that Rashmir must have promoted her when he took the throne."

The gruelling climb finally ended without any mishaps. Passing through an arched recess, the group came across a large statue in the middle of the cobbled courtyard. It stood tall and proud, with a spear placed in one hand and a shield in the other. The face had unfortunately bore the worst of the weather, with the eyes and mouth of the statue's face starting to wear away to nothing. Yet, the shiny metal inscription on the bottom gave the impression it had been recently replaced. Written in the italicized scrawl of Elvish, it was up to Leonhard to translate it to the rest of his team.

"Here lies the bones of Geriante Hassein, the first of his name," he read. "Known collectively as Geriante the Great, the fabled warrior prospered in the second Elvish Civil War of 1806, thereby creating the Hassein dynasty. Long may his spirit watch over the royal forest of Ilsthyr."

"So this is the famous Geriante Hassein," Ella said, breathing heavily. It was her mother who had once been a great lover of history. She had told her daughter the famous story of Geriante using black magic to defeat his enemy, Raymond Falkijr, instead of hand to hand combat. Repeating such rumours here though would result in Ella being thrown in the dungeons, or probably worse.

An elderly guard then approached the squadron leader and saluted with both hands. "Good to see you, Frau Helga," he spoke in the Elvish tongue. He glanced at Leonhard and diverted his attention away just as quickly. "His highness is currently in the council chamber."

"Very good," she replied, no hint of breathlessness in her voice. "Are we all prepared?"

"As ready as we'll ever be, my lady." He gestured to the two guards behind him to open the heavy set doors.

Leonhard knew the soldier to be Adlebert Faust, head of one of the most powerful families in Ilsthyr. As a child, Leonhard had often played with his younger son, Torren, in the halls of the palace. To a young Leonhard, the palace seemed enormous and he was forever getting lost. Now he had grown up and seen more of the world, he realised it was not much bigger than the academy at Northwood.

Despite this, Adelbert said nothing to Leonhard, moving to the other side of the courtyard instead. Deep down, Leonhard wanted to plead with him that he had no part in the Luthai's death, but knew his words would be wasted.

'I am as much as a traitor in their eyes as my father,' he thought. *'At least I didn't get spat at this time...'*

The Hassein coat of arms of a bow and arrow in front of an orange sunset hung proudly above the two towers, flapping in the wind. Once through the postern gate, Frau Helga led the group through the high beamed entrance hall with its double staircase. Portraits of previous Hassein monarchs adorned the walls of the hall. Luthai's collection of rifles had been taken off the walls and stored away. Instead, new additions to the decor included flamboyant chandeliers and strange wicker sculptures that were hard to distinguish. Rashmir was indeed transforming the place into his own.

A chorus of voices drifted from the end of a long hallway. The group found the council in session; ten elves all sat around a long pine table with King Rashmir in the centre. The vaulted chamber opened out onto an ancient sulphur bath with steaming hot springs. At that moment, Leonhard would have given anything than to dive in the lime green water and wash the dirt away from his grubby body.

A ruby studded crown was nestled in the midst of the young monarch's curly black hair and he wore a closely cropped beard. Engaged in deep conversation, he failed to notice Frau Helga enter the chamber.

"The crown has repeatedly placed the trust in his business," the King said, looking at each of the councillors in the eye.

An elf, at least three times Rashmir's age, nodded in agreement and at once rolled out a piece of parchment. "Whilst I must agree with you, your highness, Lord Visyr has stated that he will not contribute any more workers to the cause until he has been paid what is owed."

The King looked even more resentful. "And what is that?"

"Ten thousand gold marks, plus two thousand in interest," the councillor said. "The debt has apparently accrued over your late father's reign, your highness."

"My father wouldn't have allowed a debt to be unpaid! Send a letter to Lord Visyr and invite him for a meeting. Failure to attend will renounce all of his family's lands and titles forthwith."

A sly smile spread from the corner of the councillor's mouth. He bowed his balding head, almost in a mocking way. "At once, your highness."

Rashmir stretched and let out a big yawn. "Forgive me, loyal councillors, I feel I have taken too much of your time already. Before I adjourn the meeting, have we any other business?"

Frau Helga abruptly strode past one of the pink blossom trees that flanked the chamber and stood over the far side of the table.

"I do, your highness," she said, giving a customary salute to the King.

"Frau Helga, it is good to see you again," Rashmir said. He leant over and poured her a cup of an unusual thick purple liquid. "What news do you bring?"

"We found four trespassers at the edge of the forest." She took a brief sip of the juice out of respect and grimaced as she swallowed. Whatever the drink was, it certainly wasn't to her liking. "They had set up camp and were armed, your highness. The young elf claims to be Ruven Solveig's son."

Intrigued by her words, Rashmir clapped his hands and drew the meeting to a close. The councillors each bowed and left the chamber, save for a young elf at his side. He wore the same cloaked armour as Frau Helga, but looked only a boy. By the way he had remained in the room, Leonhard decided that Rashmir had already found a replacement for his father.

"Odin's breath, it is you!" The King ran over to Leonhard and embraced him like a long lost brother. "Welcome back to Ilsthyr, Leonhard!"

Surprised, Leonhard struggled to breathe from the King's firm grip. "A lot has changed, I see."

The young King laughed, showing rows of perfect teeth. Rashmir had been a gallant prince, melting the hearts of many women in his youth. Ilsthyr's population loved his easy going nature and good sense of humour. "Ha, you are not wrong! I'm sure it's been a long journey from Northwood. Would you and your friends like to sit and have an elderberry juice with me?"

Leonhard accepted the invitation. "I'm sorry for your loss, your highness." He then introduced the rest of his party to Rashmir. The King responded by shaking each of their hands in turn and announced his bodyguard was named Herr Willen.

"I have heard a lot about you, General Martine," Rashmir said. "My father spoke highly of you."

"He did?" Martine asked.

"On a number of occasions. I hope you all weren't mistreated by my soldiers?"

"Erm...they were quite forceful," Leonhard said, telling the truth.

Meanwhile, Finn flushed with anger. "Forceful?" He pointed towards Frau Helga, who stood casually against the far wall. "One of 'em hit me in the back of my head!" He rubbed the back of his skull, as if to reinforce the point. "It feels really bruised! I've probably suffered brain damage and god knows what else!"

Rashmir glanced at the woman sternly. "Is this true?"

Frau Helga said nothing, looking slightly amused.

"On behalf of my soldiers, I do apologise," Rashmir said. "My orders to them were to apprehend any outsiders who were in the vicinity of the forest. We cannot be too careful at the moment."

"What is going on, your highness?" Martine asked plainly, lighting up a cigarette. "It looks like you are preparing for a battle."

"I'm sorry, we don't allow that 'activity' here," he stated, scrunching his face at the approaching smoke. "My guards can escort you out of the city if you wish to continue smoking."

Martine looked around the room, expecting the joke to reveal itself. When he realised the King was deadly serious, he reluctantly stubbed the cigarette out with a grunt. "Any wine then?"

"I'm afraid not. Having seen what the drink did to my father, I refuse to touch the stuff." Rashmir took a sip of his elderberry juice and licked his lips bitterly. "So, you were asking me what is happening, Mister Martine? Shortly after my father died, my sweet sister declared herself for the throne."

Leonhard couldn't believe what the King was saying. "The Princess Davini?"

"The very one. She left the city, eager to gather forces to support her false claim. We heard reports of her in the area, hence why I sent out a group of soldiers to scout the royal forest."

Davini had always seemed a kind and good natured woman. If the new King told it true, it seemed totally out of character.

"Why would she do such a thing, your highness?"

"Please Leonhard, you've known me long enough to call me Rashmir." He then crossed his arms. "According to Davini, it was my father's wish for her to take the throne. It is folly, of course. He would have never supported her succession. No woman has ever ruled Ilsthyr."

Leonhard surveyed the room, noticing both Frau Helga and the King's bodyguard were eagerly listening in. "Can I ask you about what happened with my father?"

Rashmir nodded, understanding what Leonhard was getting at. "Frau Helga. Herr Willen. Please, can we have the room?"

The young guard looked somewhat dumbfounded by the King's request and peered at the mercenaries suspiciously. "I must protest your highness! It might not be safe to leave you unguarded, considering after what has happened recently."

The King ignored the young guard's protestations, spouting a short, sharp laugh that sounded like a bark. "I think I will be quite safe, Willen." He winked at Leonhard. "You aren't planning to kill me, are you?"

Leonhard thought the joke surprising, especially after what his father had been accused of. "No...not at all," he said.

"There, see? Willen, please check on the battle preparations with Frau Helga. I will see you later."

Grudgingly, he did as he was bid. As the guard left the room, King Rashmir brushed Herr Willen's hand and their eyes met for a brief moment. It was over in a second, but the room saw it.

'Are they...lovers?' Leonhard wondered. *'King Luthai would turn in his grave if he had found out his son was in a relationship with another man.'* He saw the disgust on Frau Helga's face and knew their relationship was no secret.

King Rashmir only answered Leonhard's question when the clink of Helga's armour became distant.

"Herr Ruven was found standing over my father's body in his bedroom," he said. "He was holding a bloodied knife that had been used to stab the King repeatedly in the stomach."

If Rashmir felt upset over his father's death, he didn't show it. He spoke rather nonchalantly, as if murder was somehow an everyday occurrence.

"It still doesn't mean my father killed the King," Leonhard said, biting his bottom lip. He tried to play the scene through in his mind. "He could have been set up."

"I agree."

"Wait! You do?"

"Yes. Your father served the King faithfully. More than that, they were good friends. I have tried to find a motive for murder, but I cannot come up with anything. My true belief is that Herr Ruven was in the wrong place at the wrong time."

Leonhard swallowed through his dry throat. He reached for the elderberry juice and downed it in one. It was a little sweet for his taste buds, but still quite refreshing.

"Is there any clue to where my father would have gone?" he asked. "We need to find him to find out what happened."

"I wish I knew," Rashmir said. "He was unfortunately long gone by the time I heard the news." He heard Leonhard's cry of dismay and sought to justify himself. "I know you must be eager to find him, Leonhard. I would lend you some of my soldiers to assist you, but I need all of my forces here in case my sister returns."

Leonhard knew the King meant well. He could understand that Rashmir's immediate priority was to defend his claim to the throne. There was a sibling squabble going on here and he feared how far the young King would be willing to go.

Yet, he couldn't help feeling they had wasted a journey in coming to Ilsthyr. General Martine had thought it would give them answers, but it had only raised more questions. Scraping the chair across the stone floor, he started down the corridor in a huff.

"Leonhard!" the King called. "I have just had a thought."

He paused. "Go on."

"I said 'I' didn't know the whereabouts of your father." Rashmir grinned and tossed him a heavy bronze key. "I do know someone who might, though."

Thirteen

Rashmir instructed Leonhard to leave his bow and arrows in the palace, whilst telling the rest to remain until they returned.

"Please, feel free to look around my humble abode," he said, placing a luxurious looking green silk cape over his shoulders. "Make yourself at home!"

General Martine had lived long enough to know when a gesture contained a hidden meaning.

'Feel free to look around...as long as you don't step outside my walls!'

Martine had only seen the flamboyant elf once before on a visit to Ilsthyr, plucking a four string ukulele and singing to a crowd of onlookers outside the Holy Temple of Odin as a boy of ten. It was clear that Rashmir enjoyed a crowd and always lapped up the attention he received. The General had always hated a show off.

"I do feel it would be better if I went with Leonhard," Martine argued, having to look upwards to speak to the King. "Especially if he isn't armed."

Rashmir shook his head firmly.

"We are heading into the Temple, Mister Martine. It is a sacred place where weapons are not permitted. No harm will come to us, I assure you."

The General stood in a tense silence, gazing coldly at Rashmir. He then glanced at Leonhard, who waited impatiently at the end of the room. He instantly felt powerless to change the situation. It was like a splash of cold water in the face.

This wasn't the academy. He wasn't in charge here.

"I have your word?" he ultimately said.

Rashmir grinned and clapped him on the back. "You worry too much, Mister Martine! We will not be long."

Martine sank back into his chair, feeling defeated by the naive King's words.

'If you saw the things I had seen, then you would learn to worry too,' he thought. He watched anxiously as the pair walked around the cloister, emerging on the far side of the bath and out of sight.

With his hands held proudly behind his back, Rashmir led Leonhard up a twisting stairwell. As one of the housemaids exited a room on the third floor, the King called out to the young woman in a jovial voice.

"Please be a dear and see that our distinguished guests have some food brought to them," he instructed.

"Yes, your highness," the white capped maid replied shyly. She attempted a curtsy that needed more practise, almost tripping over her own feet. With her face as red as a tomato, she lifted her black and white skirt above her ankles and hurried on down the stairs.

At the topmost floor, King Rashmir unlocked a set of double doors and traversed his way across an incredibly narrow corridor. Even with his and Leonhard's lean physiques, the walls pressed close at their sides. Anyone one much larger, say for example the previous King would have gotten themselves stuck for sure.

When it seemed like the walkway would never end, daylight flooded the darkness. The view from the top of the palace was awe-inspiring. The scenery was filled with a plethora of reds, browns and greens as the woodland dominated the landscape. The residents using the walkways below looked like tiny ants going about their business. At a guess, Rashmir and Leonhard must have been at least a thousand feet above the forest floor. In the far distance sat a range of mountains coated in white.

The breathless beauty ended there though. An abrupt blacktop of a highway split its way through the countryside like a hideous twisted scar. Even from miles away, the monotonous drone of human traffic threatened Ilsthyr's peace and tranquillity.

"You can almost smell the fumes," Rashmir said, his nose twitching like a rabbit. Now they were alone, he was speaking back in the Elvish tongue. "My father allowed the humans to build a train station here, but he always thought that damn road was a step too far."

He started across the iron bridge that linked the palace with the Holy Temple. As he walked, the arches creaked under his feet.

"Come, Leonhard. Time is short."

Leonhard had been focusing on a wooden hut to the left of the bridge. A very pretty female elf was looking out from the upstairs balcony. She ran a hand through her curly blonde hair and spotted Leonhard gawping at her. About to raise her hand to wave back, a male elf, presumably her partner, appeared behind her and ordered her inside.

"I see you have quite an eye for the ladies, Leonhard," Rashmir jested. "Like that young woman you travel with, for instance. What's her name?"

"Ella" Leonhard said, apprehensively. "And we're just friends."

"Really? I only met her half an hour ago and have already noticed the way she looks at you. The way she yearns for you!" Rashmir then winked at Leonhard. "Love is our true destiny, my friend. We do not find the meaning of life by ourselves alone. We find it with another."

Leonhard let the King walk across the bridge, his green cape blowing in the wind. The King was well known and often derided for liking the finer things in life, but to Leonhard's knowledge, the elf had always been in relationships with women. In fact, he recalled that Rashmir had been promised to a daughter of one of Ilsthyr's wealthy families and was to marry once the girl had reached adulthood.

Standing on the steps to the Temple, Rashmir raised an eyebrow. "I see you want to ask me about Herr Willen, right?"

Leonhard turned his head slowly and glared at the King. It was as if he had read his mind.

"He only came into my service a short time before father was killed. I took to Willen very quickly. He made me feel safe and alive. When he is at my side, I feel I can do anything. More importantly, he made me realise I had been living a lie all of these years."

"It can't last though, Rashmir," Leonhard said, pointedly.

"May I ask why?"

"Because...you are the King. You are meant to marry and create little princes and princesses. Heirs to your throne. That's what Kings do."

"Pfft, there is plenty of time for all that! My father frequented with whores aplenty, even when my mother was alive. Kings are allowed to have some fun too, you know."

'He doesn't realise how serious this is,' Leonhard realised. Frau Helga's expression was still vivid in his mind.

"The more people know about your relationship with Herr Willen, the higher the chance that someone would use that information against you. Your sister, for instance."

"So tell me Leonhard, why does it matter to you? You left Ilsthyr for a better life, or so I have been told."

"Because this is still my home and I do not want it turning into a war zone. Especially when there are more critical things going on in the world at this present moment."

The King softened his stance. "What things? Please tell me."

So Leonhard did. He started with the Sleima mission and Salamander's betrayal. He told him how his blood had resurrected the Sorceress from her lifeless state and described Salt's new army.

Scratching his head in bewilderment, the King put the pieces together quickly. "That would mean this Leona related to you," he said.

"My father's sister," Leonhard confirmed. "My aunt."

"If that is the case and she is as dangerous as you say she is, why do I have no knowledge of her?"

Leonhard was secretly glad that wasn't just his father who had kept things from him. Telling Rashmir everything that had happened had made him feel slightly better, like a weight was finally off his shoulders.

"Her death happened before the both of us were born," he said. "Both of our fathers probably thought it was water under the bridge. Either way, I need to know where he is before it is too late."

A deep moat surrounded the temple which emptied into the river below via a gushing waterfall. To the rear, a tumbling cascade of sandstone rocks led down the hillside towards Ilsthyr's residential area, allowing the smallfolk to enter the building for daily prayer. Rashmir and Leonhard carried on up the gleaming white steps towards the columned Temple entrance. The golden domed roof loomed high above them, shining brightly in the sunlight.

"It is a thing of beauty," the King said. "However, first appearances can be deceptive." He pointed directly above their heads at a chevroned arch. "My stonemasons carried out a survey of the Temple and found six parts of it in need of repair. Can you see that large crack, Leonhard?"

Now it was mentioned to him, it was fairly obvious. Small chunks of blue and white tile had broken off and shattered at their feet.

"It appears the movement of the land underground is causing the decay of the building fabric," Rashmir continued. Passing through the doorway, he acknowledged two elves who bowed to their King in return. "I'm not too worried though. The Temple has weathered the elements on this hill for nearly a thousand years. I'm sure it will stand for many more to come." He looked around and lowered his voice. "When this business with my sister has been resolved, you and your General have my support for the battle against the Sorceress. Humans and Elves will fight together to defeat this evil, I swear."

Leonhard thanked him with a hint of trepidation in his voice. Even with the Elven army at their backs, Salt's force still outnumbered them greatly. And they had been trained with weapons that could serve an incredible amount of damage. Going into battle would literally be bows and arrows against the lightning.

The spicy smell of burning frankincense inside the Temple failed to mask the nervous tension that filled the air. The wooden pews were sparsely populated, with many of Ilsthyr's residents busy preparing the defences of the city. A woman with a milky glaze over her eyes raised her head at the sound of approaching footsteps and stared inquisitively at them. She gave no indication if she actually saw her King walk by her as she lowered her head just as quickly and began rocking back and forth in her seat.

A mother and son did acknowledge their monarch however, bowing in appreciation. Ever the charmer, Rashmir kissed the woman on the hand and patted the young boy's blonde locks.

"My neighbours are saying Princess Davini could strike at any moment," she said, clasping her trembling hands behind her back. She took a step backwards, staring at her feet. "Do you think it will come to war, your highness?"

The King placed a hand on the nape of her neck, making her stiffen slightly. "What is your name, my dear?"

"Heidi, your...your highness."

He crouched down to the boy's level. "And your name, son?"

"Yannick!" he said confidently. "If there is a battle, I want to fight!"

The boy's proclamation of bravery made the King laugh until tears started to his eyes. "I'm sure you do, little Yannick. If only all my soldiers had as much spirit as you!" His voice became softer still, yet more serious. "I want to reassure you both that fighting is the last thing I want. Hopefully, my sister will come to her senses and things can go back to normal. Please, I don't want you to worry."

Heidi seemed to take comfort in those words and she smiled back in relief. "We won't. Thank...thank you, your highness! May the gods watch over you!" She folded her hands in prayer and led her son out of the Temple.

"Was any of that the truth, Rashmir?" Leonhard whispered afterwards.

"Not a bit of it. If Davini thinks I will give up my throne easily, she has another thing coming."

The stone altar was crafted into a twenty five foot statue of Odin, the wisest and most powerful god in the Elvish religious texts. With a strong pout on his chiselled face, the God stared fixedly at those who would enter his palace. He stood stiffly, with a spear in front of his muscular upper body.

Odin's hard face had scared Leonhard as a child. Even now, he felt the God's blank eyes follow him as he walked around the Temple. Instead, he focused on four stained glass windows that surrounded the altar. Each window portrayed the four stages of life according to Elven religion;

introduction, growth, maturity and decline. These stages were represented by four minor gods who served Odin in the afterlife. Throughout their history, Elves had made it their custom to pray to these five Gods in order every day, usually in the evening. Rashmir lit a candle and placed it next to the hundred others at Odin's feet. He knelt beneath it and mumbled a prayer. Leonhard was about to do the same when a sizeable shadow fell over them and spoke.

"Your highness! I wasn't expecting you here until later this evening."

The moon faced elf behind them was clothed in a white and gold robe that fell to his ankles and a pointed hat that hid the bulk of his bald head. Rolls of fat bulged underneath his neck and swung from side to side as he spoke. He wore a multitude of gold and silver rings on his chubby fingers. "Shall we make our way to the confession room?"

"I have many sins to confess, High Priest Finfl, but not to you!" Rashmir said in a surprisingly rough manner. "Me and Leonhard here are heading 'below'."

Momentary panic swelled on the Priest's face. "Yes, yes. Of course." He looked nervously over his shoulder. "I...I will be right back."

"Heading below?" Leonhard enquired, watching Finfl disappear into a side room.

"There is a network of ancient tunnels that were built long before this Temple," Rashmir said. "They lead to the guardian of the Earth Crystal. If anyone knows where your father would have escaped to, it would be the guardian. I really don't know why I didn't think of it before."

So General Martine was telling the truth. The mythical crystals did exist. Leonhard's hands shook with a nervous excitement.

High Priest Finfl returned a few minutes later, waddling his large legs towards them. He wiped the dripping sweat away from his cheeks with a white towel and again looked timidly over his shoulder.

"Please, follow me."

The priest drew back a pair of floral printed curtains that were suspended behind Odin's statue and beckoned Rashmir and Leonhard into the hidden room. Stopping before a stone pulpit, Finfl mumbled a brief prayer and dipped his pudgy finger into the holy water. He drew a circle on each of their foreheads and held out an identical rusty key to the one that had been handed to Leonhard.

"Do want to do the honours?" Rashmir asked.

Leonhard took the key out of his pocket. Now he knew what it was for, it seemed to weigh twice as heavy in his hand.

"I don't know what to do," he confessed.

"There is a keylock on either side of the stone," the priest said in between heavy breaths. "We rotate them counter clockwise at exactly the same time to gain entrance to the chamber. On my count. One, two, three!"

As both elves turned their keys, the floor began to vibrate beneath them. The pulpit came apart with a scraping sound to reveal a sweeping stairwell. Heavy dust rose up and hung motionless around the room, making Leonhard cough.

"You will be needing these," High Priest Finfl stated, handing them two lit torches. "Odin watches over you, your highness!"

The glow from the lit kindling barely illuminated the inky darkness as the two elves descended the dank stairs. Sounds of trickling water became more profound as they neared the bottom. Rashmir led Leonhard down a straight corridor towards a T-junction. The coral blue water that ran on either side of the moss covered pathway, along with the cracks in the ceiling made the light levels more bearable.

"This maze was built to catch out the unwary," Rashmir said. He held the torch under his face in a way that made his comely face look distorted and skull-like. "Rumour has it that Dagomir Hussein, Geriante the Great's youngest son, played a game of hide and seek down here with one of his friends. The unfortunate prince was never found. His spirit is said to haunt these corridors, still searching for his way out." He reached for Leonhard's jacket sleeve and yanked him close. "Let us not end up the same way as poor Dagomir, ok?"

Leonhard gulped, trying not to think of it. "You better lead the way then."

Rashmir took the first right and followed the corridor around a bend, approaching another junction. Worryingly, it mirrored the previous one exactly in length and appearance.

"How is that possible?" Leonhard asked. In the General's office, Martine had told him that Freya had to undertake a challenge before she reached the crystal's guardian. He guessed this must be it.

"I wondered the same the first time my father took me down here," Rashmir said. "The trick is to keep turning right where possible."

They did this three more times and finally reached a square chamber. Light shone through a narrow slit in the middle wall, showing to them the outside moat. King Rashmir walked across to the left hand side of the room and highlighted to Leonhard a small winch on the wall, with an exact replica opposite.

"We need to turn these wheels clockwise to divert the water and release the drawbridge," he shouted. "Only then can we reach the Guardian."

Leonhard brushed the cobwebs off the right hand winch and gripped the handle hard. It didn't budge.

Using both hands this time, he bent his knees and pulled with as much strength as he could muster. He could feel the veins pulsing in his neck as he gritted his teeth together. Finally, it began to loosen and Leonhard was able to turn it. Water streamed through a grate in the floor and carried on underneath their feet. A dozen rotations later and a faint crash signified the drawbridge was in place.

Leonhard leant against the wall, catching his breath. His sharp ears picked up another noise that sounded like the rattle of drums.

Bang! Bang! Crash!

Goosebumps made his hair stand up on end and he felt his blood run cold. "What is that?" he whispered. He suddenly became very jealous of Finn, Ella and General Martine back in the relative safety of the King's Palace.

"The guardian's army has awoken," Rashmir said. "We need to hurry!"

The incessant banging reached a deafening crescendo across the dripping drawbridge and then stopped. Leonhard could still hear the ringing in his ears as he climbed through the passageway at the end onto a suspended balcony.

Beacons of fire had been lit in the crypt, illuminating the room in a scarlet glow that gave the impression of stepping into the gates of hell. He looked down in awe as a colossal army of grey and flecked green terracotta warriors stood perfectly still, spears at their side.

King Rashmir let Leonhard descend the stairs first, closely inspecting the soldiers. He watched from above as the elf ran his hand across the intricate armour of the nearest one, his fingers feeling the crevices of the soldier's helmets and breastplates.

"They're just statues!" Leonhard proclaimed, the relief evident in his voice.

"Are they?" Rashmir said, behind him. "Tell me then, where do you think the noises came from?"

Leonhard concentrated on the soldier nearest to him, leaning in closer. The austere expression on the face gave nothing away and he couldn't detect a heartbeat in the soldier's chest.

It was when he moved the back of his hand to the nape of the soldier's neck that Leonhard recoiled backwards in horror. The ceramic texture was hot to the touch. How was that possible? He studied the sandy floor and saw the dozen impressions that the soldier's long, thin spear had made.

"I don't understand. What are they?"

Rashmir sauntered past him and walked between the columns of the army.

"The guardian's infantry," he said. "The militia of the fallen. They have been called many names throughout our history, but believe me when I say this. They are alive and they know we are here!"

Leonhard grimaced. It was as he walked away from the fighter that he saw its body move out of the corner of his eye. He heard the scrape of its feet on the ground and the heavy clunk of the armour. It was now facing him in a threatening stance, his spear outstretched.

Out of habit, Leonhard reached for an arrow behind his back and immediately condemned himself for acting foolish. He had no weapon with him.

"Don't do anything to provoke it, Leonhard," Rashmir said, speaking very slowly. Disconcertingly, the King's previous confidence had diminished. The way he was now acting suggested that the army's actions were different this time. Why was that? The King crept forward, his hands up in the air. "It sees you as a threat, nothing more."

"Nothing more? I thought you..."

Leonhard froze his speech, noticing the soldiers at Rashmir's back were standing in the same pose. They were now surrounded and more importantly, defenceless.

"They won't attack us unless their Guardian orders them to!" Rashmir directed his torch towards a stone tunnel. "Let's go!"

Leonhard's legs felt as stiff as posts.

"How can you be so sure?" he said, his voice barely audible. He dared not take his eyes off any of the statues.

"Trust me, Leonhard!"

Leonhard forced himself to take the King's outstretched palm and swing one foot in front of the other. He tried to ignore the loud scrape of armoured heels along the floor. Instead, he concentrated on two stone plinths either side of the tunnel that led to the guardian of the crystal.

The walkway between the army started to narrow. Leonhard knew that in any moment, they both would be swallowed up, impaled on all sides by the jagged points of the soldier's weapons.

With a mighty grunt, Rashmir pulled Leonhard's arm and leaped high into the air, landing with a crash ahead of the first row of warriors. Both rolled away in opposite directions, each receiving a faceful of sand. King Rashmir winced as he drew himself up, clutching his right arm. He turned just as the army closed up the walkway. Each soldier withdrew their spears once more and remained completely still, as if nothing had happened.

Dusting himself off, Leonhard widened his eyes. "You could have gotten us killed, Rashmir! What were you thinking bringing me down here?"

The King shook his head sharply, feeling slightly abashed. "I don't understand it. Whenever my father brought me to see the guardian, the army would let us past with no resistance. Something is different this time, Leonhard. You must believe me."

"Well they're annoyed by something and I don't want to stay to find out what it is! Tell me, how far is it now?"

"We head through the tunnel. The Earth crystal awaits us on the far side."

The tunnel ran through a series of arches and sloped upwards. Rashmir's torch illuminated a series of Elvish logographic scripts that covered its walls. The earliest diagrams, portraying the founding of Ilsthyr and the first Elvish King were still remarkably intact. Scholars had since added interpretations of each monarch's reign to the wall, some more crudely drawn than others. It was a fantastic insight into the tumultuous history of the Elvish race. Glory, war, treachery, murder and infidelity all had their place there.

A young looking Luthai Hassein had been sketched at the end, standing next to a skewered boar. Leonhard knew Rashmir's father had been a revered hunter in his youth, so he actually thought the diagram apt. He then pondered how history would portray the young elf standing next to him.

"Finfl drew that," Rashmir said, his voice sounding low and resigned, pointing to the last sketch. "He and my father were inseparable once. I blame him for introducing father to the drink. And the whores." He kicked the wall, the sound echoing through the enclosed space. "It's a shame I have to put up with him as the High Priest for another six months."

"Why don't you just remove him then? You are the King!"

"You are right, I should." Rashmir looked over Leonhard's shoulder, satisfied they weren't being followed by the terracotta warriors. "Yet Finfl is a powerful man with his fingers in many pies. My councillors would be outraged if I forced him out of the position." He stroked his beard, as if in thought. "No, he can stay. My father didn't teach me much, but I do remember him once saying to keep my friends close and my enemies closer. I intend to do just that."

As Leonhard placed his first foot forward into the room at the end of the passageway, an extraordinary white light emitted from a circular symbol on the floor. The wild sound of thunder broke the stillness, crackling onto the heavy walls. Leonhard shuddered at the sound, shielding his ears from the swirling noises that cascaded around him. He tried to scream, but he never heard a sound escape from his throat.

It was only when Rashmir tapped him on the shoulder that Leonhard opened his eyes again. He stood speechless for a long moment, stunned at the great mass of the mud-brown coloured Earth crystal that had appeared in the centre of the room.

"Rashmir Hassein," a sharp animal-like voice called out. It sounded so close that it made Leonhard jump with alarm. "I suppose I should congratulate you on your inheritance to the throne."

"Thank you, Volos," Rashmir replied hesitantly, his eyes searching the room. "I have brought somebody with me. This is..."

"...Leonhard Solveig, Ruven's only son," the guardian finished for him. "Yes, I have been expecting him."

"You...you knew my father?" Leonhard asked, not sure in which direction to speak to. The voice sounded so clear in his head. Was he imagining it?

"Yes, young one. He came to see me several times. The more apparent question would be why." He changed his tone to something more direct. "But that's not why you are here. You want to know where he has gone, correct?"

"Yes, yes I do. Can you tell us?"

"No."

"What?" Leonhard couldn't believe it. Yet again, more knockbacks. With an instant bitterness building inside him, his vision turned glassy. "What do you mean no?"

"To tell you what happened and where your father has travelled would take too long. Time is short...for all of us. It would be easier to show you."

Rashmir frowned. It was clear he hadn't any idea of what the guardian of the Earth crystal meant.

"Tell us what to do then," Leonhard sniffed. His voice was demanding, as his patience was wearing incredulously thin.

"Step towards the crystal and touch it. The both of you."

Although an element of mistrust was written across Leonhard's face, he did as he was told. He and Rashmir paused before it and waited for the count of three. They each held their facing hands to the jagged points of the crystal and observed the white light start to swirl between their fingers.

A tingling sensation rose up fast and hard in Leonhard's body. The ends of his toes and fingers felt numb and his heartbeat slowed to a steady pace. Through the dazzling light, Leonhard thought he saw the shadow of a black creature lurking in the background. He tried to pull his body closer towards it, but his actions only served to increase the distance.

Leonhard turned around. There was only whiteness. King Rashmir was nowhere to be seen.

'Is he experiencing the same sensation as me?'

Leonhard called out to him, but his voice sounded flat and empty. There was no echo in this place.

None at all.

"Close your eyes Leonhard," the voice commanded.

"Why?"

"I cannot show you unless you relax your whole body. Close your eyes!"

'This is ridiculous. What am I doing here?'

Still, Leonhard remained quiet and still, letting all thoughts escape his sceptical mind. It was only then that he subconsciously sensed his body being sucked into the black whirlpool of time, hurtling towards the truth of the past.

Fourteen

The scene slowly fitted together like a jigsaw puzzle. Gone were the bright natural colours of the present. Instead, the world was cast in a strange sepia tone, from the pre-dawn sky outside the room Leonhard was standing in to the intricate pattern of the rug that covered the rushes. His nose picked up a peculiar musky odour that was unlike anything he had smelled before.

A great mass of a man snored loudly in the corner, with the bed sheets rising high with his deep breaths. A flagon of red wine was perched on the bedside table, three quarters empty. Leonhard looked around the room, expecting to see Rashmir next to him. He had touched the same crystal after all and like he had, had surely been transported into the past. But here Leonhard was, all alone in the room with the snoring man.

He had no idea if he was playing a mute bystander, watching the sequence unfold in front from afar or if he was actively involved. He decided to inch slowly forward, being careful not to wake the man. As he loomed over the bed, Leonhard saw he had an abundance of thick matted hair that covered his pointed ears. Even as the fat elf slept, he recognised him at once; King Luthai Hassein.

'I've returned to the moment before his death,' he realised, feeling strangely exhilarated.

Leonhard reached over to Luthai's wine glass and attempted to pick it up by the stem. His fingers went straight through the glass as if he was a ghostly entity. All of a sudden, the animal-like voice spoke up again inside the depths of Leonhard's head, confirming his suspicions.

"The past has already been written," it snarled. "You cannot interfere into what has gone before."

Incessant rapping on the door roused the King from his sleep. With a hand to protect his sore head, Luthai scanned the room briefly and hit the pillow once more.

Another series of knocks followed, this time louder and more urgent.

"Wha...What? What is it?" Luthai managed to clamber up into a sitting position, rubbing the sleep from his eyes.

There was no reply from the person on the other side. Only more knocking that served to shake the door.

"Come in, damn you!"

Again, silence. The King threw the covers to one side, revealing soiled white underclothes. Leonhard moved to the far side of the bed as the King stumbled towards the door, groaning and cursing under his breath. He wrapped a dressing gown over his exposed body and reached for the handle. "This better be important," he mumbled.

A black robed figure stood on the other side of the doorway, with the cloak too loose to pick out any redeeming features. The dim light hid the person's face from Leonhard, but the King seemed to recognise the person.

"Oh, it's you," he said. "Why did you not enter when I told you to?" He regarded the person's robe. "And why are you dressed like that?"

As Leonhard moved closer for a better view, he spotted a sudden flash of silver. A cry of pain engulfed the bedroom as a knife was plunged deep into the King's stomach. Pools of blood quickly spread from the protruding hilt, staining his gown a dark red.

The spectre of death seemed to sense somebody watching, inclining their head in Leonhard's direction. They didn't wait for Luthai to hit the ground, instead fleeing the scene at once.

'That's not my father,' Leonhard thought, noting the garish way the disguised figure had left the room. He or she had moved with purpose and intent.

Luthai had recognised the assailant. It had to be someone else on the inside, seeking to profit from the King's death.

Leonhard stirred just as quickly, aiming to follow the murderer down the gallery. His progress was halted at the doorway however, with an invisible barrier blocking his path.

He watched as his father came flying into the room a moment later, wearing only the black cuirass of his leather armour. Judging by his scruffy hair and unkempt appearance, Ruven had only just woken himself from the room opposite. The last time he had seen Leonhard, Ruven had admitted he had been more often than not sleeping at the castle. He said he had felt lonely in the house by himself, with his only son away at Northwood's military academy and his wife long gone.

Ruven now stood over his King's lifeless body, rubbing at his eyes in disbelief. Leonhard could sense the alarm starting to swell within his father, a temporary paralytic fear gripping his senses. Here was the monarch he had sworn to protect and had given his life for. He had failed his duty and allowed him to die on his watch. Ruven slammed his fist to the ground in anger and threw his head back, tears coursing his cheeks.

Leonhard could see his father weighing up his options, mind bubbles concealed from sight. In his agitated state, Ruven paced over to a dressing table in the far corner and pulled a large white cloth from the drawer. He knelt over King Luthai's body and carefully prised the blade away from his hairy stomach, wrapping the cloth around the fatal wound to act as a dressing. The knife had turned ruby red, with matted blood dripping onto the rug.

With his attention completely fixated on the weapon, Ruven never heard the approaching footsteps. Leonhard knew what was coming. He shouted for his father to run before it was too late. There was no response.

A smattering of guards piled into the room, their eyes darting between the dead King and the knife in Ruven's hand.

"Step away and drop the weapon, Herr Ruven!" one demanded. His accusing eyes were as sharp as an eagle.

Ruven snapped out of his trance, raising his brow at the soldier.

"The King has been murdered!" he said, his tone still shocked.

"I said step away and drop the weapon, Herr!"

"Are you accusing me, Herr Gareth?" Ruven replied, his puzzlement quickly turning to anger. "I heard his highness scream out. By the time I got here, the murderer had gotten away!"

He then noticed the doubt on the faces of the three guards.

"For goodness sake, I was the one that trained you! And knighted you! What reason do I have to kill the King?"

Herr Gareth stood, torn between loyalty to his mentor and justice.

"Herr Ruven...drop the weapon and come with us." His edgy fingers moved towards the grip of his spear. "Or we will be forced to act!"

"You wouldn't dare!"

Each soldier had now raised their spears and stood threateningly.

"In the name of his royal highness, King Luthai, protector of the Kingdom of Ilsthyr, I am apprehending you on the charges of regicide. Herr Ruven, I will ask you to drop the weapon for the final time, or face the consequences."

With his mouth gaping, Leonhard counted the seconds of tense silence. It was exactly as Rashmir had predicted; his father had been caught in the wrong place at the wrong time.

Ruven's gaze flickered between the window and the corridor behind the elves, weighing up his escape options. He regarded the King with sadness and finally spoke up with fury.

"This is madness! I will not be charged for a crime I didn't commit. As the King's royal bodyguard and your old commander, I am now asking you all to drop 'your' weapons!" He held the gory knife out in a challenge. "Or face my consequences!"

Herr Gareth acknowledged the threat, his lips smiling at Ruven's lack of armour. "We will take our chances." He turned to the two guards. "Herr Tytil, Herr Quarik, seize the traitor!"

Watching his father move swifter and with more power than the elves half his age made Leonhard's heart swell with pride. Ruven quickly disarmed the soldier nearest to him, striking the blunt end of the spear at the vulnerable part of his throat. There, the soldier collapsed to the ground, coughing and spluttering from the blow.

The second lumbered forward, jabbing his weapon aimlessly at Ruven's chest. It lodged itself harmlessly in the grooves of the chest plate of his cuirass, allowing Ruven to spin and land the blood soaked blade he still held into the soldier's right calf muscle.

Herr Gareth scrunched his face in annoyance. With his dark eyes blazing, he twirled his own weapon around as if it was as light as a feather and darted forward. Spears clashed end on end, with both sets of feet dancing too fast for Leonhard to keep up.

Herr Gareth may have been mentored by his opponent in the past, but the cocksure young soldier now applied some of his own tricks that were at odds with Ruven's clean and honest approach. As Gareth pushed him back towards the unmade bed, the soldier stuck out a leg, tripping Ruven over.

Leonhard's father saw the incoming spear just in time and rolled his body in a full three hundred and sixty degrees rotation.

The move served to annoy Herr Gareth further. He spat out like a boiling pot, reaching over and hurling the dead King's wine flagon at Ruven. The aim was all wrong however, sending it towards one of the windows instead. Panes of glass shattered into a thousand pieces.

Ruven could hear approaching reinforcements and now sensed his escape route. His adam's apple bobbed upwards in his throat as he nervously glanced at the jump he would have to undertake.

"Stand and fight, you coward!" Herr Gareth spat, drawing his spear once more.

"I promise I will fight you, Herr." The sounds of footsteps grew closer to the room. "Just not today." Ruven pivoted his body towards the gaping hole in the glass and jumped.

The scenes that followed were a series of snapshots of his father's escape. Spending no more than a few seconds in each, it felt as if Leonhard had entered a picture book and someone was flicking the pages to show him the story. The first displayed Ruven sneaking over the stone walls of the Royal Palace, tumbling down the hill into the town. The sun hadn't yet risen over the trees and luckily for him, the majority of Ilsthyr's residents were still abed. The sense of shock in his father's body had now been overtaken by a steely determination to get clear.

The scene went fuzzy, fading entirely.

The action was picked up again seconds later, this time deep into Ilsthyr's woods. Leonhard spotted a solitary eagle perching on the stone roof of an ice house, the bird of prey plucking at its coarse feathers with its beak. The remains of a mouse lay at its feet, with only a string of the rodent's guts still to be eaten. It's head pricked up at an approaching sound, with it's personal grooming seemingly interrupted. As Ruven came crashing through the undergrowth, the eagle took off, not bothering to gather up the last of the helpless rodent. Maybe it would swoop down again once the threat had passed.

Ruven had escaped the immediate danger of the town and afforded himself a quick breather. He made water against the side mound of an ice house, totally unaware that his son from the future was standing close behind. He zipped himself up quickly, the sound of his panting magnified in the quiet of the forest. It only took a distant snap of a branch to set him on his feet once more, aware he was still being chased.

As the location switched before him, Leonhard was relieved to see his father had gotten clear of the woods. Ruven knew the path through the forest better than most and would have been sneaky enough to have backtracked several times to confuse his pursuers. Now, he was threading through fields full of rapeseed crops that dazzled despite Leonhard's burnished vision. His father had acquired a grey jumper from somewhere and now wore it over what little armour he had, pulling the hood over his head to stop him being recognised. The path through the fields descended dramatically towards a small port at the banks of the sea, with a small monastery out in the distance. Checking behind him once more, his father started towards the town.

The final clip revealed Ruven halting before the base of a series of mountains, taking in the sheer height of it all. Night had come, with layers of fog clinging to the snowy crests. Raindrops were falling, drumming on the hard ground.

In his curiosity, Leonhard held his hands out to collect a pool of water. The droplets fizzled out to nothing before they hit the surface of his skin.

His father had been travelling for a number of days and it showed. The stiff movement of his legs resembled nothing more than a limp. His eyes were bloodshot and his lips had become dry and cracked. With columns of fire acting as a guide, Ruven followed a twisting pathway upwards towards a stone pergola. It was as he disappeared into the mountains where the visions concluded.

"So you're the guardian?"

The dazzling light rescinded quickly. Once more, Leonhard stood facing the rotating Earth crystal, firmly back in the present. An enormous wolf-like creature prowled around its base, watching him curiously. Swirls of brown marked its white fur, extending from the snout to the lower reaches of its back. The creature then faded from view, appearing again near the wall. "You sound surprised?" it said back.

Leonhard blinked repeatedly. He couldn't hide his astonishment. How could something move like that? And now the wolf creature was talking! Talking!

"I thought you might be...well, like me."

The wolf grinned almost wickedly, baring rows of sharp-edged teeth. "An elf? No! My brothers walked this earth long before the first elf settled in these lands. I've seen generations come and seek my enlightenment and observe the magic of the crystal." It stretched out its long front legs and treaded towards Leonhard. "Come now, I'm sure you have questions for me?"

"The final vision that I saw? Where was that?"

"The dwarven kingdom of Kahr Dovidor, deep in the Morodir mountains," a third voice came in. This one was more amicable and easy-going than the guardian. It was King Rashmir, appearing from the tunnel behind Leonhard. "Don't worry, I saw what you saw, Leonhard. Your father is a smart elf. Considering our history with the dwarves, it would be the last place we would consider looking."

'*Smart, indeed,*' Leonhard thought. '*And dangerous.*' "Tell me this then, is he still there?"

"Yes," the guardian said. "But it would be wise not to dawdle. He will be on the move soon."

"Where?"

"My visions into the future only go so far. I cannot say."

The guardian silently watched Rashmir and Leonhard leave. They retraced their steps through the labyrinth, with the return journey being a lot less eventful than before. The army of the dead had created a narrow pathway for Rashmir and Leonhard to pass through, remaining motionless this time. As a security measure, the King proceeded to haul the drawbridge back up, sealing off the cave and the crystal once more.

"Your father didn't deserve to die like that," Leonhard said to him, walking through the last set of tunnels. "Did you happen to see who killed him?"

"No," Rashmir replied, gritting his teeth together. "The murderer fled the city before I could give chase. Volos did tell me that I will find out who did it very soon though. Tell me Leonhard, are you leaving straightaway?"

Leonhard nodded once. "You heard what the guardian said; my father will be on the move soon. I need to find him before that happens."

"In that case, take one of my boats. Follow the river to the town of Port Isaak. You will reach it quicker than your father did. Kahr Dovidor is not far from there."

"Thank you, Rashmir. That would help us. I can't promise I will return the boat, though."

"I wouldn't expect you too," Rashmir answered in a friendly voice. He paused, breathing in the dank air. "All I ask of you Leonhard is that you would consider joining the Royal Army after you have finished your time at Northwood. You wouldn't just be a regular soldier either; I would make you a Commander!"

He noticed Leonhard looking stunned. "Well, say something!"

It was true that Leonhard felt flattered by the King's proposition. He hadn't really given much thought to his future career beyond Northwood. Here and now, Rashmir was giving him a title and a position of honour in the Elven army.

Still, Leonhard had his doubts.

"I am only sixteen," he said. "Your men wouldn't listen to a young elf like me!"

"And I am only twenty, Leonhard. Age has nothing to do with it. We both know that your father was wasted as my father's bodyguard. He had an exemplary career in our army because he was a fighter at heart. Forgive me for saying this, but your mother's death killed some of that fire in his stomach. But you have that same fire, I know it! You don't want to be living with humans for the rest of your life, right?" Rashmir's eyes twinkled as he waited for a response.

"I don't really know what to say."

"What does your head tell you?"

"I would be honoured!" Leonhard said finally, accepting the offer with a hearty handshake. "Does this mean that I have to start calling you 'your highness' from now on?"

That brought a ripple of laughter from Rashmir which reverberated down the passageway. "Our fathers were good friends. I want us to be too! As I have said before, a simple Rashmir will do."

With the matter resolved, the two elves carried on through the final corridor. Bright daylight shimmered at the top of the staircase and it took a few moments for Leonhard's eyes to adjust.

High Priest Finfl stood restlessly at the base of the pulpit. Panic gripped his large face and he tousled at his robes apprehensively. Something had clearly happened since they went below.

"Your highness, I am so relieved that you have returned! I heard voices below and knew you would be near."

Rashmir didn't need to ask what the problem was. Looking over the priest's shoulder, he noticed Frau Helga standing at the entrance to the temple along with a hundred armed retainers.

She started towards him. General Martine, Finn and Ella were also there, their faces grave.

"I tried to tell them, your highness, I did," Finfl continued. "They should know weapons are forbidden in our sacred temple, but your lady Commander refused to listen to me. She demanded to know where you were."

"I will sort this, Finfl," Rashmir said. "Your worshippers will no doubt be panicked by this. Go to them. Reassure them that everything will be fine and to carry on as normal."

"Yes, at once. May Odin give you strength!"

The High Priest walked clumsily towards the pews, scowling at Frau Helga as she marched past him. Her face also spoke of urgency, but Leonhard noticed something else there too. A hint of a smirk, perhaps? Whatever had occurred, she was secretly enjoying it.

"Your highness," she said formally, bowing her head. She regarded Leonhard with the same look of revulsion as before.

"Could this have not have waited until we returned?" Anger was clear in the King's voice. "You all of people know what the penalty is for carrying weapons here."

"I do. And I am sorry." Her tone suggested she wasn't. "We have a situation."

"What kind of situation?"

"It's your sister, your highness. She is at the city gates with an army at her back. She demands that you meet her or she will attack!"

Fifteen

The sudden news made Rashmir storm out of the Temple, his face as black as thunder. Herr Willen waited patiently outside on the steps, helping the King into his slim fitting armour before handing him his weapon.

The double bladed spear Rashmir was holding was extremely unusual to Leonhard's eyes. The hilt had been crafted from thick ivory with a moulded grip and the two asymmetrical blades had been forged into a wavy pattern. It was an impressive weapon to behold and clearly made the other soldiers in Rashmir's army slightly envious. Yet, Leonhard couldn't but help to notice how immaculate the blades looked, immediately absent of chips and scratches.

'Has Rashmir even fought in a battle before?' he wondered. He had a sneaking suspicion that he was about to find out.

Ilsthyr's residents lined the walkways, watching with apprehension as the royal procession marched towards the city gates. Among them were Heidi and Yannick, the mother and son that had approached the King in the Temple. Watching the King stride by from the doorway to their hut, the child attempted to squirm free from his mother's firm grip. Rashmir briefly locked eyes with Heidi and his face instantly turned red with shame. Her strained expression spoke louder than words ever could.

'You lied to me!' it seemed to say.

The shadow of guilt caused Rashmir to walk with his head down, daring not to meet any of the other watching eyes.

Adelbert Faust awaited the King at the gates, saluting at once. He, like the other soldiers, had sheathed himself with the lightest armour he could get away with on an increasingly muggy autumn day.

"We have the Princess Davini and her forces surrounded, your highness," he said assuredly, pointing to the archers on the wooden ramparts above his head.

"How many does she have with her?" Rashmir asked directly.

"No more than fifty."

"Fifty?" He turned inquiringly towards Frau Helga, who shrugged her shoulders. "I thought you said she had an army with her!"

"Well, what exactly constitutes an army?" she asked.

"More than fifty! Herr Adelbert, have your men load their bows. I want their spears at the ready in case my sister decides to breach the city walls. Fire only on my command!"

Leonhard watched Herr Adelbert climb the battlements with astonishment. The soldier really was going to go through with the King's orders. Had the world suddenly gone mad? As the King signalled to open the city gates, Leonhard knew he had to stop this sibling feud before it spilled out into an all out war.

"Rashmir!" he called, pushing his way past a stunned Frau Helga. "What do you think you are doing?"

Either the King hadn't heard Leonhard or he was being ignored. Rashmir placed his foot on the first step that would take him down to a meeting with his sister.

"Wait, please!" Leonhard persisted, tugging hard on the King's emerald studded gauntlet. "Don't do this, Rashmir! You heard what Herr Adelbert said. You really think she had come to attack with just fifty men?"

Rashmir's eyes flashed angrily. "Why are you still here, Leonhard?" he spat, ignoring the question. "I thought you were leaving straight away."

The King's reptilious scowl had hurt him. Yet, Leonhard tried his hardest not to show it. "Not until you tell your men to lay down their weapons."

"Are you serious, Leonhard? Take a look over them walls, I urge you! Fifty men or not, you really think she would do the same? No, you don't know my sister. You don't know what she's like."

"No, you're right," Leonhard said cautiously. "I don't know her. But I know you. This isn't you."

Rashmir's lips quivered. His eyes flickered between Leonhard and the archers above. He then noticed Frau Helga, standing impatiently and eager for battle.

"I have no choice," he whispered in a voice that sounded boyish. "You think you know me, but you don't really. You don't know me at all."

Leonhard's stomach sank as he watched the King and his army stride down the same steps he had been forced to walk up this very morning. It seemed like a lifetime ago. Not even a reassuring pat on the shoulder from General Martine helped alleviate the frustration and fear he felt.

"There's nothing more you could have said," Martine said. "The King's mind is made up. We should all go whilst there is still time."

Leonhard heard a flutter of wings from the nearest tree and spotted two doves take off into the sky. He saw it as a sign, which filled him with a vain hope. He turned back towards the town.

"Not yet, sir. There is something I need to do first."

Rashmir met his sister on a patch of scrubland that was carpeted by fallen leaves, with the two flanks of soldiers watching on. General Martine had decided not to follow Leonhard. Along with Finn and Ella, he worked his way through the orderly lines of Rashmir's army. Amongst the steely scowls and grunts they endured, the General noted the smell of fear emitting from the younger soldiers. He had been in the same position once. Their stomachs would be tied up in knots as they anxiously waited for what would come next. Arriving at the front column, Martine managed to catch the first words between the two warring siblings.

"Is that really you I'm speaking to, sweet sister?" Rashmir asked, screwing up his eyes. "You do sure look different."

Martine had seen Princess Davini at a passing glance only once on a visit to the Elven kingdom. She had only been a child then, no more than twelve. Yet, he had noticed something different about Davini even then. It was a refusal to conform to the traditional norms of an Elven woman, especially in the way she dressed and acted. She wouldn't be satisfied by marrying a rich lord's son and raising his children. No, Martine could tell from that brief moment that she demanded more from life. And now here she was, a decade later, claiming her father's seat on the throne.

Davini's blonde hair had been shaved at the sides and styled in the middle as a mohican, most unlike an elf's traditional haircut. She wore a sleeveless armoured top that highlighted her bulging biceps and had marked her cheeks in black face paint. Standing with an armed force at her back, it made her look rather intimidating to Martine.

"Some things change, Rashmir," the Princess started in a harsh, wispy tone. She turned her head sharply towards Herr Willen. "And then some things don't. Answer me this, Rashmir; would your men still follow you if they knew about your lifelong profanity as I have?"

Rashmir's fingers twitched around the hilt of his spear. She was belittling him by challenging his sexuality. "They will follow me because I am their rightful King!"

"You didn't answer my question."

"I don't need to. You might be of my blood, but you defied my rule when you left. Unless you have come to beg forgiveness, I should have my army execute you and your ragtag force for treason."

Davini appeared unmoved by the threat. "Look behind me, brother. Does it look like I have come to bend the knee?"

Shielding his eyes with one hand, he contemplated the young men and women at her back with a mild smirk.

"I am struggling to see what your intentions are, I really am. Fifty soldiers, pah!"

His smile then dropped as he recognised a familiar face amongst Davini's troops. "Lord Visyr, is that really you?"

A mean looking elf with a horseshoe style haircut came forward, positioning himself besides the Princess. His yellow eyes resembled that of a snake, with two keyhole shaped black pupils positioned in the centre. He chose to ignore Rashmir's question, answering it by an irate frown.

"My councillors and I were only talking about you this very morning in our meeting," Rashmir continued. "By the looks of it, it seems like they told me old news. You were scheming with her all along, right? Behind the back of your King?"

The Lord again said nothing, with his scarred face bearing a sly simper.

"Lord Visyr joined my cause because he believes in my claim," Davini added, speaking for him. "He isn't the only Lord I have the support of."

"Hmph, is that right? Where are these Lords you speak of then? I don't see them."

"Then you aren't looking hard enough, Rashmir."

A brisk trepidation soared through the King. He hadn't a clue what she had meant by that last sentence.

"I've heard enough!" he cried, the resentment clear in his voice. "I'm giving you one last chance to end this madness and disavow your false claim. Or you and your men will suffer the consequences."

"Why should I? I am the elder sibling. The throne is mine by right!"

"By right?" Rashmir snarled, his words forced through clenched teeth. He shook his head so furiously, it made his crown tilt to the left of his head. "You have no right! You are a woman, unless you have somehow forgotten. No woman has ever ruled Ilsthyr!"

"Just because it hasn't happened in the past doesn't mean it can't happen now. Father desperately tried to reach out to you, but he knew from a young age you preferred gallivanting over politics. So he turned to me instead. He let me sit in his council meetings. He let our Weapons Master teach me how to fight. I even represented the King at the last Continental Congress meeting when he was too hungover to attend." She pointed an indicative finger at him and raised her voice. "So don't tell me that I have no right just because of my sex! I am a stronger leader than you ever could be!"

Rashmir looked to the heavens, as if waiting for a sign. His mind was seemingly made up.

"I knew it would be a waste of time talking to you, Davini," he ultimately said. "You've always done what you've wanted, without a care for anyone else but yourself. You made a mistake coming back here. This is my time now, my kingdom! I will not let you ruin it!"

He raised his left arm into the air slowly. The archers on the wall responded by aiming their bows squarely at Davini's army. At a guess, Martine thought the distance was a little over a hundred metres. It was a distance where they couldn't fail to miss.

Rashmir took one last pitiful look at his sister and turned back towards his army. Frau Helga gave him a dutiful nod. He halted as Davini asked him one more question.

"Are you sure you want to do this, Rashmir?" If she was fearful of impending doom, she didn't sound it.

"Yes," Rashmir said quietly, his back to hers. "Yes I am." He started to lower his hand...

"Hold it!"

The Royal Army turned towards the source of the shout and split across the middle. Rashmir became visibly traumatised as he watched Leonhard march towards him, together with hundreds of Ilsthyr's civilians. The elderly men, women and children all created a barrier in front of an impassive looking Davini.

"What in Odin's name do you think you are doing?" Rashmir cried, spittle flying in all directions.

"A good King listens to his people, Rashmir," Leonhard said.

He then turned and addressed the crowd he had gathered. "I ask you all now! Do you wish to see this petty feud come to war?"

The resulting cry back was defiant and resolute. "NO!"

"If you order your men to fire at the Princess, then they will have to first kill the people you were sworn to protect at your coronation. Tell me Rashmir, would you be able to live with that?"

"Leonhard, this...is...madness! As your King, I am ordering you all to move clear! Now!"

Ilsthyr's residents stood as motionless as the army of the dead Rashmir and Leonhard had encountered not an hour before. General Martine, Finn and Ella joined the protest, angering the King even further.

"We aren't going anywhere," said Leonhard. "Disarm your men, Rashmir!"

"And then what? The next thing you'll want is for me to lead her to the palace to discuss peace terms."

Leonhard nodded. "That's exactly what I am asking."

The only sound came from an unexpected gust of wind. Both forces stood nervously, uncertain of the outcome.

Knowing he had been beaten, Rashmir finally gave the signal to stand down. He rubbed his face with a heavy sigh. "I hate you for this, Leonhard."

Leonhard returned a smile. "You gave me no choice. What do you say, Princess?"

Looking at her brother with a sense of loathing, Davini clapped a firm hand on Leonhard's shoulder. Her stare was ice cold.

"First, you will tell me who you are, 'little' elf?"

Leonhard found her phrasing quite derogative. It was as if she was sending him a message that he shouldn't have interfered.

"Leonhard," he replied simply.

"Leonhard, whom?

How did she not recognise him? She must have seen him countless times around the royal palace with his father.

'I was even sitting no less than five seats away from you at the Moonlight Festival.' Then he thought *'maybe it's the beard.'*

As Leonhard informed her of his surname, Davini's dark features brightened. Her eyes perked up with interest that made him feel slightly uncomfortable.

"Fine, I will grant her safe passage to the Palace," Rashmir said. "We will talk alone and unarmed." He regarded Lord Visyr with a bitter stare. "The Lord and his men will remain outside the city where they belong. If nothing is agreed within the hour, I will call my banners once more. Do you agree to these terms, Davini?"

Her eyes were locked on his. For one agonising moment, Leonhard thought his intervention had all been for nothing. Davini then carefully handed Visyr her spear.

"I do," she said. "You had better lead the way."

Sixteen

A solemn looking grandfather clock ticked away in the corner of the palace study. The passage of time was marked by the slow swinging of the brass pendulum, descending back and forth in its rotation. With his head in his hands, Leonhard looked again at the clock face.

'Quarter past six. We've been waiting here for two hours now,' he realised with a groan.

Two hours had passed since he, Ella, Finn and General Martine had been bundled into the room, followed by two soldiers. One stood guarding the door, whilst the other sat messing with his hair by the small window.

The air inside the small room was close and airless. Straightaway, Leonhard felt damp pools spread underneath his arms and had repeatedly asked for the window to be opened. It had been met with a harsh silence.

'I've potentially saved us all from civil war and now you are keeping us prisoner,' he thought miserably. He watched a green bottle fly do a lazy circuit of the room before landing back on the table.

'The fly is as bored as we are.'

With his ear pressed against the wall, Leonhard and the others had tried to listen to the conversation taking place across the hallway between the two Hassein siblings. It had started with raised voices with both announcing their displeasure with each other. A quiet spell followed. After a while, the talking had resumed at much calmer volume and in the last few minutes, there had even been one or two instances of laughter. Leonhard knew the omens of a resolution were now more positive, but painfully hoped it wouldn't take too much longer. He badly needed a drink and embarrassing grumbles came from the pit of his stomach.

"Have ya got a problem with me?"

From out of nowhere, the sound of Finn's voice made Leonhard's heart skip a beat. Feeling puzzled, he looked across to see his friend giving the door guard an evil look.

"Why should I have a problem, human?" he replied back.

"Well, you keep on starin' at me. I wanna know why?"

The elf guard raised his eyebrows towards his friend near the window and turned back to Finn. "I don't have to answer to a 'coward' human like you."

Finn leapt out of his chair so fast that it sent the stool tumbling to the floor. "Say that again, I dare you!"

Leonhard thought there had been something familiar about the guard from the minute he had shut the door. Now, hearing how he spat the word 'coward' confirmed it for him.

"It's Herr Gareth, isn't it?" he asked the guard.

"Wait, you know him?" Finn asked, fists poised.

"Not personally, no."

Leonhard walked over for a closer look at the guard's face. Although his chestnut brown hair was wilder than before and now tumbled to the back of his neck in a mullet style haircut, it was definitely the same man. "You fought my father, didn't you?"

"Yes I did," Herr Gareth said honestly. "Or at least I tried until the traitorous scum fled."

"He's not a traitor, Herr. He is innocent! The King was stabbed by someone else in a cloak. He tried to tell you but you wouldn't listen."

"And how would you know this?"

Leonhard wondered how much he should tell Herr Gareth of his encounter with the Earth Crystal guardian. The crystal's presence in Ilsthyr wasn't common knowledge. If he told Herr Gareth it had transported him back into the past, would the soldier believe him?

No, probably not. He would regard Leonhard as crazy.

"I saw it in a vision," Leonhard put it simply.

"Is that so?" Herr Gareth asked, arms crossed. "I frequently have visions at night too. In them, I'm married to seven women. Each one of them adores me and obeys my every command." His joke drew a snigger from his friend in the corner. "Then I wake up and realise that I only have one wife. She doesn't obey me. All she does is nag day in, day out until it drives me insane."

"This was different. This was real." He saw the sceptical look across both of the guards faces. "Ask King Rashmir if you don't believe me! He saw it too. He knows my father didn't kill King Luthai!"

At that moment, several footsteps sounded down the hallway. Herr Gareth moved himself away from the door just as the handle started to turn.

"Apologies for the delay, my friends," Rashmir said breezily, stepping into the room along with Princess Davini. Herr Willen and Frau Helga hung back outside, clearly at odds with one another. "I'm sure you will understand we have had a lot to discuss about the past. And the future."

He turned towards his sister and beamed at her.

"In light of recent events in Ilsthyr and outside, we have decided to call a truce and share the power. We will sit on the throne together!"

Rashmir clapped Leonhard on the shoulder before anyone had a chance to respond.

"It's thanks to you that this was possible," he continued. "To celebrate this momentous day, I have decided to throw a party!"

Herr Gareth tutted disapprovingly that went unnoticed by the King.

"And when do you exactly plan to hold this celebration, your highness?" the soldier asked.

"This very night!"

"But there isn't enough time. All the Lords and Ladies of the realm will need to be notified!"

"I agree, Herr Gareth. Go to High Priest Finfl and tell him to ring the bells three times. Make sure it is three, whatever you do. Our lords, ladies and the smallfolk will listen to our news and party under the stars!"

He turned to Frau Helga. "Notify the kitchen team to check the provisions. The last time an inventory was done, we had enough food to last us until spring." Finally looking like the excitable young prince Leonhard had remembered from his youth, Rashmir rubbed his hands with glee. "Yes, I have an overwhelming feeling this is going to be a night to remember for us all!"

The news of the imminent party spread quickly throughout the royal palace. It became all hands on deck; the kitchen staff hastily prepared the food and drink, whilst the housemaids, stewards and gardeners made sure the guests could be accommodated inside and outside the palace.

With so many of the household staff displaced from their usual positions, Finn thought it an apt time to explore the palace further. It might be his last chance, as Leonhard had informed him of his intention to go northwards at first light to search for his father.

Finn had found Ilsthyr peculiar, immediately noticing a lack of modern technologies that he had taken for granted growing up in Northwood. It was like he had stepped into a time machine and gone back three hundred years. For the majority of Ilsthyr's residents, running water was scarce, electricity didn't exist and the only way to get around the city was by foot. Before today, he had thought the elves he would meet would be as friendly and accommodating as Leonhard. This hadn't been the case. Many of them had wrinkled their noses at Finn like he was a bad odour. It gave the impression of the Elves believing themselves to be somehow superior to humans.

He knew enough history to know that their society still functioned through an outdated, and once thought extinct, feudal system. Here, the monarch still reigned supreme with absolute power, with the Lords ruling over the smallfolk. Houses differed in all shapes and sizes, with the lower classes living in no more than wooden shacks. Women were definitely second class citizens here too, simply fulfilling the role of raising families and looking after the household for the man. Only time would tell if the situation would change with Rashmir now sharing the throne with his sister.

Still, for all of its faults, there was something pure about the Elvish way of life. Ilsthyr seemed far removed from the stresses and strains of modern human cities. It was quiet, the air was clean and the elves seemed at one with nature. The residents took pride in their city, with rubbish and graffiti nowhere to be seen. Even though he had only been here a day, it would be strange for Finn to return to normality once more.

He found himself traversing down a corridor on the topmost floor of the palace. The patterned carpet rotated back and forth in a blue and white geometric pattern. Staring at it for any length of time sent him dizzy. He tried to touch the ends of the expensive looking chandeliers, but the tips were too far out of reach. It was no wonder; he and Ella were the smallest people here by far. Even General Martine must have felt short in this place.

Finn tried the first two doors nearest to him. They didn't budge. The third did, however. He twisted the iron handle in his palm and the door opened with a heavy creak.

The room before him was magnificent, yet too excessive for his simple tastes. A mahogany oak four poster bed dominated the centre, draped in lace. Rich tapestries adorned the walls. The air inside was fragrant with the smell of lavender. And above the bed hung a large portrait of the owner of the room, standing proudly on the carcass of a dead deer. It was then that the door clicked shut.

"How do you like it, then?" King Rashmir stood, arms folded. He had changed out of his armour into a navy studded jacket, complete with a mustard yellow cape around his shoulders. His eyes slowly looked Finn up, down and up again. His right eyebrow was arched in an almost lascivious way. "Normally I wouldn't let strangers into my room." A wicked grin lit the King's face. "I might make an exception for you though."

Finn bit his lip, feeling uncomfortable under the King's seductive scrutiny. He knew at once it was a mistake to be wandering this strange place, all alone. His palms became clammy. His gaze searched the room, daring not to meet the King's eyes. He badly needed a distraction.

"What...what are these?" Finn then asked, noticing four haphazard structures perched at the side of a dressing table.

"Hm? Ah, they are called Fortune Totems," Rashmir replied. "It is an ancient elvish tradition that dates back thousands of years. Elves would have them in their homes to ward off evil spirits and it is rumoured to give the owner luck for the year ahead. Pick one up if you like."

Finn knelt and inspected each statue in turn. They measured around three feet in length. Different animals that inhabited the forest had been eloquently carved into the wood and had been painted in a multitude of colours. The gnarly bark of a tree ran through its middle, with each twisted groove translated almost perfectly. An eagle sat on its top, wings spanned as if it was ready for take-off. He picked up the nearest one to him and was surprised how light it was.

"What do you think to them, young man?" Rashmir asked.

Finn thought them rather odd, but didn't dare say it to his face. "Yeah, they're not bad, I 'spose."

Rashmir laughed. "Not bad? That is high praise indeed coming from a human! Credit where it is due, I would no doubt find some of your traditions strange too. I will just have to work harder next time."

Finn straightened himself and placed the statue back down. "You're sayin' that you made these?"

"That's right. It is a secret hobby of mine. Only Herr Willen and a couple of my household staff know that I make them. I learnt the skill of woodcraft from my great-Uncle. You see, he was fourth in line to the throne, so had to find other ways to assert himself. He ran a highly successful artisan business here in the city. I respect him a lot for prospering in the face of adversity."

"What will you do with the ones you've made then? Sell 'em?"

"Ha! Can you imagine me with a stall in the marketplace trying to sell them to the small folk? They resent having to pay their King taxes. I doubt they will part with any more of their coin for my benefit!"

Like a heavy cloud blocking the sun, Rashmir suddenly became sad and despondent. "I want you to take one with you."

"Why?" Finn asked, eyes wide.

"Because the path you seek will be long and arduous. Leonhard has told me what you are up against and I have promised him I will help. If it gives you just a small portion of luck, then it will be worth it."

Finn nodded. "Ok. Thanks, I guess."

A long arm shot out towards him, which he duly shook. It was as he tried to pull clear that he felt Rashmir harden his grip.

"I want you to promise me one thing, though."

Finn could feel the bones crunch in his hand. He gasped, shocked by the elf's strength. The wish of wanting to be anywhere else returned to the forefront of his mind. "Fine, name it."

"I want you to promise me that no matter what happens, you will stick by Leonhard."

"Of...of course I will." Who was he to question his friendship? "He is my best mate. Wherever he goes, I go."

The tension abruptly eased. Finn flexed out his aching hand. He could make out the white impressions the King had made underneath his thumb and little finger, slowly fading to a more natural pink.

"I'm glad to hear it," Rashmir replied absently.

Hearing a chorus of laughter from the terrace below, he moved past Finn towards the window.

"Ah, my lords and ladies have arrived!" The King's words became hushed, almost as if he was speaking to himself. "I will first make a speech announcing the new developments. Yes, the applause will be deafening! All will agree that this was the only way forward. I will be hailed a hero. The common folk will admire me even more than before. They will cheer until..."

"Er, King Rashmir?"

Snapping out of his trance, Rashmir laughed.

"Yes, forgive me. It has been quite a day, hasn't it?" He stopped himself before the door and turned. "Don't forget to take a Fortune Totem. And please, close my bedroom door after you leave."

Staggering back to his feet, Leonhard knew at that moment he had drunk too much of the sweet mead. He had initially refused the first drink placed in front of him by Torren Faust, one of his childhood friends. Alcohol had never been something that had appealed to Leonhard. His father had taught him all about the perils of the stuff. First of all, a person would slur their words. Then, your actions became confused and you would end up making a fool of yourself. Finally, if you had consumed too much, then you would regurgitate it back up and wake up with an extremely sore head the next morning. Even though he was now at an age where there was peer pressure amongst his old friends to try it, Leonhard honestly didn't fancy it.

"One sip, that's all I ask," Torren had pleaded with him. Leonhard's friend didn't share the same proud eloquence as his important father and had always spoken with an annoying nasal voice. Permanently dark eyelids gave Torren a jaded look and his lips drooped dismally even in high spirits.

Leonhard noticed Torren was half way down his third tumbler already. "Haven't you had enough already?" he asked him.

"The night is still young, Leonhard!" Torren had replied with a wink. He slid the glass closer, acutely aware of Leonhard shying away from it. "Anyone would think I've given you poison. It's mead my friend, that's all."

Leonhard had eventually concurred, partly to silence Torren's annoying insistence. It had been a short sip, but he felt the mead immediately satisfied his taste buds. He particularly liked the sweetness of the honey on his lips and he quickly went in for more.

Before Leonhard knew it, his tumbler was empty. Senses intoxicated, his vision became unfocused. His heart rate slowed and he began to relax.

"Where do you go to get them refilled?"

Torren snorted a laugh. He pointed towards a makeshift bar on the far side of the terrace. "Get me one while you're at it."

It was as Leonhard returned that he spotted Ella move towards their table. The three piece band that were providing the evening's music had unexpectedly switched to an up-tempo jig, with the female harp player preferring a mandolin for the particular number. Scores of elves crowded around the band, moving their bodies to the beat and joining hands. Leonhard felt his cheeks flush. He had been dreading a moment like this. He knew what Ella would want from him even before the words left her lips.

"Will you dance with me, Leonhard?" she asked him.

Even as a boy, Leonhard had hated dancing. He had always felt he was being watched by everybody else and would end up making a fool of himself. With adolescent sensitivity added into the mix, the prospect of walking onto the dance floor with a girl he had developed romantic feelings for scared him hugely.

Ella asked him again, concerned he may not have heard her over the thrum of the music. She held out her hand, secretly wishing him to take it.

Leonhard politely refused and sat back down again. The emotional hurt darkened Ella's face and she turned sharply away.

"You must be a fool to refuse a beauty like that," Torren said, scanning her behind as she moved. "And she's a human too."

Leonhard tutted with annoyance. Torren didn't understand his feelings. No one did.

"I haven't got time for girls at the moment," he told him.

"Why? Are you dead?"

"No. It's just that..." He bit his fingernails, debating whether to tell Torren what had happened. "It doesn't matter."

Torren exhaled a small belch and set aside his empty glass.

"I really don't get you, Leonhard" he said, shaking his finger. "She's standing alone on that dance floor and you sit here feeling sorry for yourself. You've always been a weird one."

Leonhard said nothing, attempting to look anywhere but the dancefloor.

"If you don't want her," Torren continued, "then I guess it's up to me to work my charm."

Leonhard spat out his drink at the mere suggestion. "You wouldn't dare!"

"Just watch me."

He didn't want to, but couldn't help it. Torren approached Ella and whispered something in her ear. His words had made her snigger and he pulled her closer into the depths of the crowd.

It was at this point that Leonhard felt an urge to escape the confines of the party. As he got up, he stumbled into the table, smashing the empty glasses in the process. A group of elves opposite roared with laughter. Leonhard scanned the crowd, searching for Finn or General Martine. He hadn't seen or heard from them both since they had been let out of the study and they weren't here now. Instead, he decided to escape and take a walk.

The sounds of the party were replaced by the thrum of crickets as Leonhard moved past the majestic Temple of Odin. His reflexes might have been delayed, but his feet moved as if on auto-pilot. He had walked this route back and forth hundreds of times before. He knew where he must go.

Leonhard's childhood home once stood handsomely, outshining the rest of the houses in the neighbourhood. Now, amidst the beauty of the starry sky, it looked dilapidated and unloved. The outside walls were overrun with green vines that covered the windows. The front garden had become a wilderness of bushes and overgrown weeds that gave it a strange, post-apocalyptic look.

'How could father have let it get like this?' he pondered.

Leonhard searched the garden for a wooden bucket and filled it with water from the nearby communal well. Being doubly careful not to spill any of its contents, he carried the bucket to the creaking front porch and wiped the cobwebs away from the cast iron door knob. He twisted it open and instantly felt the cool, musty air touch his face. He stepped inside.

Memories pricked his mind as Leonhard moved through the house. It had been a happy place to grow up in for the first six years of his life. He vividly remembered huddling around the fire and listening to stories from his parents. He recalled the sense of joy and wonder as he unwrapped his first bow on his fifth birthday. It was a poor thing, to be sure. The bowstring would snap if Leonhard pulled on it too hard and the arrows had its ends blunted to stop him cutting himself. Still, his father had made it from scratch and Leonhard soon realised the effort that had gone into making it.

The kitchen had always been his mother's domain. Each morning, Leonhard would wake to the sound of his mother crashing about and the mouth-watering smells of her cooking that drifted up from downstairs. She was an incredible cook and she knew it, quickly earning a reputation in the neighbourhood. Even now, he could still see her food stained pinny wrapped around her slender waist and her rosy cheeks. Seeing the kitchen bare and devoid of life made it utterly despairing.

The floorboards creaked sinisterly under his feet as he entered the small washroom. He undressed himself, noticing bruises starting to form on his chest from the battle with the Griffin and washed the dirt away from his body. His vision in the mirror became clouded by his own breath as the chilly temperature made his bare legs itch. He hastily changed into a green tunic and rested his foot on the first step of the staircase, wondering whether to venture any further.

One night in particular had scarred any previous attachment he once held for upstairs. His mother's terrible screams had started as soon as she had entered labour in his parents' bedroom. Panicked and feeling utterly helpless, his father had tasked Leonhard to brave the fierce storm outside and fetch a doctor to help deliver the baby and ultimately save her life. She and the unborn baby had died before he had returned.

His father had always blamed himself for his wife's death. Whatever had gone before was irrelevant. That night had changed Ruven and, in some ways, Leonhard too. He went outside, took one last look at the house and carried on walking.

It was only as he reached the open centre of the forest that he rested his aching legs on the dewy grass. He felt compelled to take his mind off that horrific night ten years ago and found himself singing an old elvish tune from his childhood. He couldn't remember all of the words, so filled in the blanks with his own. At the start of the third verse, he sensed a shadow lurking behind him.

"How long have you been standing there?" he asked the shadow.

"Long enough," Ella said back. She sat down next to Leonhard, her eyes glowing in the moonlight. "You do have a sweet voice, you know."

"Yeah, yeah. You're only saying that."

"No, really you do."

An uncomfortable silence followed. Ella watched him pick the petals off a handful of daisies and turned her attention to the enormous stone monuments encircling the green space. "What is this place?"

"It is where we come to bury our dead," Leonhard said. "A graveyard, as you would call it." He pointed over to the long avenue of menhirs directly in front. "The stone in the middle marks where my mother was laid to rest. The rest of my family are in the next field along. The tall stone is supposed to represent the soul's passage from this world to the underworld."

"Your mother died when you were young, right?"

"Correct. My father is all I have left now." His Aunt Leona didn't count, not at all.

"I'm so sorry," Ella said. "You must miss her so much." She traced a comforting finger around the base of his shoulder and felt him shudder. "You know, you still have people who care about you. I care about you."

"Oh really? Is that why you decided to dance with Torren?"

"You gave me no choice, Leonhard. And if you must know, it was awful."

"Awful?"

"Your friend is a creep. He tried to place his tongue down my throat. I slapped him around the face!"

"You did?" Leonhard asked, failing to hide the delight in his voice. "I would like to have seen that!"

"Then why didn't you?"

"I...I don't know. I hate crowds. I'm a terrible dancer. Just thinking about stepping onto a dancefloor with all of those people watching me makes me nervous." His eyes now held hers. For a second, he was lost in them. He lowered his voice to barely above a murmur. "You make me nervous."

"I do? Why?"

"Do I really need to say why?"

Ella nodded. She secretly enjoyed watching him try and find the words.

Had Leonhard ever felt more nervous than he did now? Sure, it had been a stressful and emotionally draining week, but this was a different matter entirely. This was love, a subject which he felt completely unqualified in. "Well, I...uh...*(come on, say it)* like you. A lot."

She continued to stare back vacantly, urging for him to go on.

"I have only known you for a short time, but…"

"But?"

"…but from the first moment I saw you, I thought you were the most beautiful girl I had ever seen. You are so fearless and…"

She kissed him mid-sentence. Running her hand through his hair, Ella felt her yearning passion grow. She felt the butterflies take off in her stomach. Her lips were intertwined with his for a moment that felt like a lifetime. She then came up for air.

"What?" Leonhard said, noticing a stray tear. Panic swelled within him. "Did I do something wrong? Did I say the wrong thing?"

She wiped her cheek and returned a wet smile. "Leonhard, you are so sweet. No one has ever said anything like that to me before, not ever. Thank you."

Now it was Leonhard's turn to kiss her. He began softly, letting the intensity build. His hands traced the curves of her body, resting on her waist. He had dreamed of this moment ever since their first meeting. His heart melted in her embrace. All of his worries were momentarily forgotten. The Sorceress, his father, Rufus Salt, Salamander; they all didn't matter at this moment.

Only Ella.

An abrupt ringing of bells sounded around them, breaking their connection.

"What…is…that?" Ella asked.

"Midnight curfew," Leonhard said, rather irate. "Why in Odin's name does it have to sound now?"

"Curfew? Man, you elves sure know how to live!" She detected his puzzled gaze and sniggered. "It was a joke, Leonhard."

"Sure, I know."

"And what would happen to us if we were naughty and broke the curfew?"

He ran a finger under her chin. He was sorely tempted by her proposition. They could get up to all sorts of things out here without anyone knowing. "For you, nothing. For me, just a step closer to the otherworld when I die."

"I'm confused. I thought you said an elf's soul passes to the underworld?"

"They do if they're good. Elves that have done wrong in their lives sink further into the depths of the otherworld."

"I see. So the otherworld is like the human version of hell."

He took Ella's hand and pulled her to her feet.

"Exactly. You wouldn't want that to happen to me now, would you?"

She pressed her body close to his and pecked him on the cheek, turning him on further.

"I couldn't bear it."

Seventeen

Leonhard and Ella found Finn pacing the beacon lit confines of the palace courtyard. He told them he and Martine had been searching the palace high and low all evening.

"You're lucky they kept the drawbridge lowered or you would both be spendin' the night outside," he shouted, sounding a little stressed.

"Now that would be a shame," Ella said, with the hint of a smirk playing across her lips. "Wouldn't it, Leonhard?"

"It would indeed," he replied, winking back.

Finn seemed oblivious to their hidden joke. "Aye, that idiot called Gareth is busy assembling a squadron to find ya both. He was particularly keen on finding you, Leonhard."

Simultaneously, Leonhard and Ella sniggered, causing a frown to wrinkle Finn's forehead. "You're both acting weird! Is there somethin' I should know?"

"Not at all," Ella said. "We're good. Aren't we, Leonhard?"

Leonhard nodded avidly. "Let's head inside before they lock us out."

The entrance hall was still, save for two armed guards standing lazily by the doorway. The invited guests had long since returned home and any signs of a party had been efficiently cleared by the household staff. Now night time had fallen over Ilsthyr, the hallways and stairwells of the palace had been lit with red candles, adding a somewhat seedy ambience.

'Definitely another one of Rashmir's little touches,' Leonhard instinctively guessed.

He and Ella started down the hallway leading towards the council chamber, hearing the crunch of their footsteps on the woven rush mats that covered the flooring. Leonhard then turned, noticing Finn hadn't followed them.

"Now this is a turn up for the books, ain't it!" Finn remarked from the top of the main stairwell. "It seems that I know somethin' you guys don't."

"Our rooms are this way," Leonhard reminded him. The quietness of the palace had made him abruptly aware of the time. He would still need to conduct his prayer duties before he retired for the night.

"It jus' so happens that I found a shortcut when I was looking for you." He beckoned them to follow with a solitary finger.

"You better be right about this."

"Have ya ever known me to be wrong?"

Leonhard searched his mind for an answer, not having to think too hard. "Well, there was that time during our practical test when you misjudged the jump across the valley and we all had to come down and rescue you. Also, you somehow got us both lost when you were showing me around the academy on my first day. Do you want me to continue?"

"Erm, not really."

"I also remember on the day of the Hardball tryouts, you boasted to all of my friends how you were once considered for the Reno Racers youth team," Ella added. "And look how that turned out for you!"

"Fine, so I may have been a tiny bit wrong in the past!" Finn said, admitting defeat. "But I'm tellin' the truth about this. Believe me!"

Ella and Leonhard trailed Finn down a tall corridor lined with gilded mirrors. It veered to the left and they all went through a set of double doors that Leonhard couldn't remember ever noticing before. Stepping onto a walkway above the palace's great hall, Finn crouched down at the sound of muffled voices below. He gestured to his friends to do the same.

"It's Rashmir and Davini," Ella whispered. "I think we should head back."

"Nonsense," Finn said. "I wanna hear what there sayin'."

"Come on, they obviously have a lot to talk about. It's got nothing to do with us." She tugged at Finn's shoulder, but he remained stubborn. "Argh, you tell him, Leonhard!"

Leonhard was burning with curiosity, eager to hear their words now the speeches and festivities had finished. It was a good sign that they were still speaking with each other, alone. Certain war had been averted today in his homeland, and he knew he should be content with the apparent peace. Yet, there was something about Davini that troubled him and he didn't know why.

"Let us stay awhile," he said.

"You're both impossible!"

"Well, we're not stopping you from leavin'," Finn said.

"You would really let a woman walk alone at this hour? No, I'm staying here with you two!"

The joint rulers of Ilsythr sat opposite each other on a long oak table, with Davini sitting with her back to the three mercenaries. The crackling fire provided the only light in the room, throwing two lean silhouettes against the wall. Decorated flowers and plants had been positioned at either end of the table and only a selection of half empty food platters from the party were now left.

With his golden crown by his side, Rashmir sat resting his palm on his chin. Davini reached over to pick up a flagon of wine and let the last drops fall into her glass.

"I will order us more," she said, talking to his brother in the Elvish language.

"To be honest, I think I've had enough," Rashmir said, yawning. His speech became slurred and his cheeks were flushed from the drink. "It's been a long day."

She waved his protests away and clicked her fingers sharply. The timid young maid Rashmir and Leonhard had encountered on the way to the Temple immediately appeared from the side doorway and nervously bowed.

"Another one of these," Davini ordered, handing her the flagon. "And two clean glasses."

"At...at once, my queen."

She snorted as the maid left.

"'My queen!' It sounds good, you think?"

"It sure does," Rashmir said casually. "You'll get used to the titles soon enough." He rose and pushed his chair away, stretching out his arms. "Seriously though, I should be leaving you to it. I'm normally not a drinker, Davini."

In truth, the wine had made the King horny and he was eager to get back to satisfy Herr Willen, who would be waiting to entertain him in his bed.

"One more drink, I promise you. We should be celebrating Rashmir! It's been a historic day, one that will go down in the history books. And it's not over yet."

"I suppose you're right," Rashmir said, sitting back down. "And then I must shut my eyes, or I will be in no fit state for tomorrow's event."

"What event?"

"Your coronation, Davini! Or have you forgotten already?"

"No, no. One final drink, I promise!"

Listening from above, Ella eagerly looked to Leonhard to translate the foreign words. Her previous knowledge of the language would only go so far.

"Rashmir was about to leave," Leonhard explained to her, "but Davini has ordered them some more wine."

"They seem to be alright with each other, don't they?"

"Yes, they do." Still, something didn't feel right.

"What's wrong?" Ella was a good reader of faces and could tell something was troubling Leonhard.

"I really don't know."

Finn had other worries to contend with. The dust from the walkway had made his nose sniffle and he had been frantically rummaging through his pockets for a tissue. He barely had enough time to stifle the sneeze with his hand before it passed through his lungs. The noise, a small expulsion of air in reality, was magnified in the vastness of the great hall.

"What was that?" Davini immediately asked, turning towards the source. The mercenaries ducked even lower to avoid being seen.

Rashmir feigned ignorance, yawning further. "It was probably one of the soldiers doing the rounds. You worry too much, Davini."

"It came from up there. I'm going to take a look."

Thankfully for the young mercenaries, the maid reappeared with the wine just as Davini approached the doorway. She regarded the wine with a keen scrutiny and instructed the maid to place it on the table, temporarily omitting the noise she had heard from her mind.

Finn glanced guiltily at his friends, whispering an apology. Hearing Davini sit down again, they each raised their heads again only when it felt safe to do so.

"You're spilling it everywhere, woman!" Davini then scorned the maid.

"A thousand apologies, my queen," the maid said. It was clear she was terrified. "I…I will be sure to steady my hand next time."

Davini was having none of it. Her shrill voice pierced through what little confidence the maid had before. "Get out of my sight! I can do it myself!"

"You were too hard on her," Rashmir said, as the door closed. "She is new and still learning. Give her time, I beg you."

His words seemed to pacify her temper. "It is good wine, that is all."

She finished pouring it and proposed a toast.

"To us?" Rashmir suggested.

"To the throne," Davini said, clinking his glass.

His eyes twinkling, Rashmir grinned at her and downed his drink in one. He scrunched his face up as he swallowed and set aside his glass.

"Tell me Davini. When you woke this morning, did you really think you would be sitting here with me drinking wine?"

"If I'm honest, no, I didn't."

"We both have young Leonhard to thank. If he hadn't intervened and made us see sense, who knows what would have happened at the city gates?"

"Indeed," Davini answered in a biting cold voice. "Where 'would' we be without him?"

Rashmir had been too intoxicated to notice her scorn. Yet, Leonhard understood perfectly.

'Davini isn't happy with sharing the throne. She still yearns for it herself.'

He could tell by her stiff posture that she was going through the motions, knowing that she would rather be anywhere else but talking alone with her brother. He leaned further over, looking around the room for clues.

'She wanted him alone for a reason. What does she mean to do to him?'

And then, lost in his thoughts, Leonhard saw it and understood fully. The untouched wine glass at Davini's side. Rashmir had swallowed his drink in one. The wine would be travelling down his oesophagus and into his stomach. A feeling of dismay grew within Leonhard and he became mute. He knew it was already too late to save the King.

"If you would agree with me," Rashmir began, "we should make finding our father's killer our first task. I visited the Earth guardian with Leonhard earlier today and saw for myself what actually happened. Ruven Solveig didn't kill the King."

"No," Davini said simply.

"No? What do you mean no? The man is innocent."

"Of course he is. However, portraying him as the murderer is easier for elves to grasp than the actual truth."

Rashmir tweaked the collar of his purple doublet and attempted to clear his throat.

"Which is what exactly?"

"I killed the King."

Rashmir coughed once with wide eyed astonishment, clasping his hands. "You killed him?" he cried, raising an eyebrow. He shoved his chair to the side and stood powerfully over her, as if he was ready to pounce. "Before I have you arrested, you will tell me why!"

Davini allowed herself a mirthless laugh and curled her lips at him. "Father always said that out of the two of us, I was the one born with brains. Isn't it obvious, Rashmir? The man had grown to be an insufferable oaf. He wasn't fit to rule this kingdom. Most days, he wasn't even fit enough to rise from his bed. You surely know this!"

"Heavens above!" Rashmir wailed, the coughing coming now in sudden spurts. He wiped the spittle away with a napkin. "It didn't give you any right to plunge the dagger into his stomach!"

"That's where you're wrong though. Ilsthyr needs a strong and committed person to rule." Now she was standing, face to face with her brother. "That is where I come in, you see. Did you really think I would share the throne with you, Rashmir? You don't have the first idea how to rule. You think it is all frolics and festivities. I, on the other hand, have been waiting for this day my entire life. I have made an alliance that will allow our citizens to prosper for eternity."

With the poison wine burning up his insides, Rashmir had to lean on the table to stop him plummeting to the floor. He held his stomach in agony, struggling to breath. Drops of blood fell from his nose, turning the tablecloth a garish pink colour.

"Frau Helga...(cough)..Herr Gareth...(cough, cough)...Herr Willen, arrest this...(cough)...traitor at once!" He gasped and fell back, hitting his head hard on the stone floor.

"They're not coming for you, baby brother," Davini said, pouring her untouched wine over Rashmir's blackening face. "Nobody is."

"HELP...ME!" he attempted to shout, but his voice had turned frail and gravelly. His hand clawed at the tablecloth, sending its contents crashing around him. With blood seeping out of every orifice, he spewed out the contents of his stomach in an awful mess. His last act in this world was to point an accusing finger at his sister, his face still contorted with hurt from her betrayal. He attempted to speak her name through the bubbles of blood that had formed on his lips, heaving his chest in defeat one last time. He then remained perfectly still, gone forever from this world.

"What...the...hell?" Finn eventually murmured, too dumbstruck to move. "She killed him!"

Ella could see Leonhard squeezing his hands together with rage. Danger was afoot. She knew it was imperative that they didn't do anything stupid that would put their lives in danger.

"We all need to get out of here," she spoke very slowly. "Right now!"

Leonhard didn't hear her. Locked in a twisted hallucination, he reached for a weapon that wasn't there and fired an arrow that hit Davini's chest. He would fire another, and another, and another. All until his quiver was empty and his revenge was served. He would then…

"Leonhard, are you listening to me?" She shook him hard, trying to catch his attention. "We aren't safe here. We must leave!"

"Shhh!" Finn whispered, finger to his lips. "Someone else is down there."

"It must have been a pleasure to watch him die, my queen."

The voice revealed itself to be Frau Helga, stepping into the orange glow. Her mouth twisted into a bitter smile as she surveyed her dead King.

It took a moment for Davini to answer. "I can't say it was. I would have preferred to do it my way, with a spear in my hand. It is often said that poison is a coward's weapon."

"A fool's speech, if ever it was. Rashmir was weak, just like his father. They both got what they deserved."

"And Herr Willen? Did he get what he deserved?"

Helga took out a bloodied blade from her leather pouch and held it up triumphantly. "He squealed like a pig when I slit his throat."

"Good," Davini said. "Take two hundred men and storm the Temple. You will need to kill the guardian and capture the crystal before sunrise."

Frau Helga bowed and left, quickly replaced by an edgy Herr Gareth.

"According to the doormen, the young elf has returned," he started. His eyes nervously flicked between his new queen and the recently deceased Rashmir. "He will have returned to the guest quarters."

"For your sake Herr Gareth, I hope you are right. I instructed you not to let Leonhard out of your sight. Find him and bring him to me! Captain Salt needs him alive and untouched. Kill the three humans!"

Above, Ella and Finn were practically dragging Leonhard across the banister, attempting to rouse him from his semi-hypnotic state.

"You heard what they said," she spoke with urgency. "We need to flee, now!"

Leonhard rotated his head heavily, his eyes wet with tears. "She…she murdered him."

"Yes, she did. And they will do the same to us if we don't leave this minute."

Yet, his body remained stubborn. "I can't let her get away with it!"

"Listen to yourself, Leonhard! Your mind is clouded by revenge! Think about the current situation for a second; we are seriously outnumbered here, we don't have our weapons and her forces know the palace much better than we do. The longer we spend here narrows down our chances of escaping." She immediately felt bad and apologised for being too hard.

"I understand you must be hurting. Davini will get what is coming to her, whether it be by your hand or not. But that time isn't now!"

It was enough to wake Leonhard from his grief-stricken slumber. "Do you promise?"

Both Ella and Finn simultaneously nodded, carefully opening the door on the far side.

Heavy footfall sounded above their heads. Leonhard knew their rooms were being searched by Herr Gareth and his outfit, so securing their things was out of the question. He also knew the front entrance would be heavily guarded, restricting their choices even further.

"Rashmir told me there was a service entrance underneath the palace kitchen that led all the way to the docking area," he said, wiping his eyes. "He suggested we use one of the boats and follow the river to a town called Port Isaak."

"Sounds a better idea than any," Finn agreed.

They moved as fast as their feet would take them, all the while remaining on high alert around each corner for any threat. Leonhard took heed of the map of the palace laid out in his head and he knew the entrance to the kitchen was within reach. They would have to traverse down two flights of stairs to reach it. Leonhard held Ella and Finn back whilst he cautiously scanned the floors below.

"What can you see?" Finn asked.

"Guards," Leonhard said, groaning softly in response. "Five of them."

"Five? Even if we had our weapons, it would be hard to get past 'em. What are we gonna do?"

Leonhard didn't need to think of an alternative. He felt his heart swell as the guards moved away from the door and out of sight. He closed his eyes and mumbled a prayer of thanks. "Now's our chance guys!"

Reaching the third step, he then noticed Finn hadn't followed. A dark figure had loomed large behind him and had a wrinkled hand wrapped around his mouth. Suddenly, the nearest candle flickered and went out.

"Let go of him!" Leonhard cried out. He felt a keen tug on his jacket and was forced against the wall.

Through the murk, he recognised the outline of a top hat and the tall collar of a trench coat. The grimy stench of smoke clung to the man's clothes, filling Leonhard's nostrils. His breathing was noticeably raspy and intermittent. Before Leonhard could speak the General's name, he felt a solitary finger press his lips shut.

"I found Herr Willen in Rashmir's room with his throat cut," Martine declared. "I looked in each of your rooms but you weren't there. Do any of you know what is going on?"

"Rashmir is dead, sir! Murdered by...Davini." Simply speaking her name sent Leonhard into a shaking rage. "She is working for Salt and the Sorceress. Everyone else here is now under her orders."

He heard the rustling of a canvas bag and was somewhat startled to find his trusted bow back in his hands.

"In that case, we may need to use these if we are getting out of here alive," Martine said, handing over their weapons. "I trust that you have deciphered a way out of here, Leonhard?"

His blue eyes blazed with pride. The General had lauded him with the utmost responsibility, despite each of their lives being on the line. It was up to him, now or never. Despite his current mood, he couldn't help but smile. He informed Martine of the plan and led the way down the steep staircase.

Leonhard hovered on the last few steps for a while, holding the others back until the danger had receded. Noticing the way their shadows danced on the beams unnerved him. It would only take a single guard to turn back and their position would be compromised. He knelt his body close to the wall and warily scanned the corridor from left to right. Three of the guards had moved out of sight. A further two stood talking at the far left side. Their words were inaudible from this distance. It seemed to Leonhard that they were waiting, but for whom?

Leonhard blew out the candle flame from above his head and instructed the General to do the same. He knew it would be foolish to linger, so he sucked in his stomach and darted towards the kitchen door. He turned the handle gradually, muffling the dull click of the latch in his palms. He applied more pressure to it, praying with all his might that no one had thought to take the key and lock the entrance to the kitchen.

Thankfully, no one had. He waved to the others to follow and closed the door behind him.

The kitchen was a dark and smoky place. Cinders from the large open fire floated through the air. The ashes still gave off an immense heat that made Leonhard feel light-headed. An assortment of metal pots and pans hung above the fireplace archway on hooks and across the width of the room. The tiled floor was still damp in places, indicating the kitchen staff had only recently finished for the evening. Martine took the dangling key from the hook and locked the door behind them.

Whilst Leonhard searched for the exit hatch, Finn rummaged through the dried goods on the central workstation. He found several loaves of freshly baked white bread and over a dozen curd pies just waiting to be eaten. He licked lips in anticipation and tore a chunk off the bread.

"What are you doing, Finn?" Ella shrieked. "Now is not the time to be standing around and filling your stomach!"

Finn had never tasted bread this good before. He was used to the pre-packed variety his mother used to buy that would turn stale within a couple of days. Soft and doughy on the inside, the bread seemed to melt in his mouth.

"We might not get a chance to eat for a while," he said, handing Ella a chunk. "Anyway, we will be needing some rations for the trip north."

"Finn has a point," Martine said. He placed his satchel on the counter and loaded it with supplies, taking a bite himself out of one of the tarts.

"Over here guys, I've found it!" Leonhard called out. He had been moving cardboard boxes around in the adjoining buttery and had discovered a trapdoor in the floor. Finn, Martine and Ella helped him clear the area, pushing the heavy food stock to one side.

Leonhard went to his knees and undid the bolts on the door. Even through the gaps in the well-worn boards, he could feel a cool draft on his face. He hauled the door open and spied the steps meandering downwards through faint light. He went first and the rest started to follow.

"Wait!" Finn froze on the top step, a sudden memory flashing in his head.

"What's the matter?" Martine called from below.

"I've just remembered that Rashmir gave me one of them Totem thingies to take with us and I've left it in my room."

"Rashmir gave you a Fortune Totem?" Leonhard said, starting back up the stairwell. "When was this?"

"Erm, jus' before the party. He said it would give us luck for our trip north and…"

"Shhh!" Leonhard's ears pricked at the sound of shuffling feet on the other side of the kitchen doorway.

"Hang on a sec!" Finn said, oblivious. "First of all, you wanted to know where I got it from and now you don't. Make your mind up!"

"Quiet, Finn!"

The urgency in Leonhard's voice finally silenced him. One of the soldiers on the other side tried the door handle several times, without much success.

"It seems to be locked," the soldier said.

"Of course it's locked," another said, undoubtedly Herr Gareth. "They are in there right now attempting to escape via the service hatch, just like I told you!"

"What do you want us to do then?"

"Let me make myself clear, Herr Morowyn. If I lose that blasted elf, the queen will tan my hide." Herr Gareth sounded irate and like a man feeling the pressure. "Before she does though, I will make sure to tell her which fool helped him and his repulsive human friends escape. I hear our new queen doesn't take too kindly to fools. Do I make myself clear?"

A chorus of voices replied in unison, understanding perfectly. Heavy boots struck the door with a number of forceful thrusts, causing a mass of splinters to break off.

Leonhard hastily closed the latch and raced down to the rest of the party.

"Is that them?" Ella asked, her features barely visible in the absence of light.

He nodded. "That door will not hold them off for long. Let's go!"

As they reached the bottom of the hatch, the atmosphere became thick with moisture. Ripples of moonlit water splashed softly against the wooden boardwalk. A seaweed covered fishing net and a rusty looking anchor had been perched against a mooring post. Leonhard scanned the boathouse at the end of the wharf for a suitable vessel, finding a modest sized rowing boat that would serve just as well as the grand barge Rashmir had lined up for them instead.

As he, Ella and Finn climbed in, the rowing boat swayed beneath their weight. General Martine untied the knot from the rope and threw them his satchel, which Leonhard caught with both hands.

"Quick, sir," he said, offering his hand.

Martine gripped it forcibly and paused. The heavy clomping of the pursuers footsteps grew louder. They would be on them at any moment. He withdrew his grip.

"What are you doing, sir?"

"Go!" the General said resolutely. "You must carry on north and find your father." He withdrew his sword and waited, his grey eyes much alight. "I will hold them off for as long as I can."

Leonhard closed his eyes in dismay. He had just watched his King die an anguishing death. He couldn't bear for it to happen again.

"Sir, this is suicide," Leonhard argued. "Get in the boat. Please!"

"No, this is what I must do. Tell your father I'm sorry."

With the current working with them, the boat had already covered a distance of thirty metres from its cast off. Finn and Ella had dropped their oars and were pleading with Martine to wade through the water.

"What are you sorry for?" Leonhard shouted.

"I promised him that I would keep you safe, no matter what. I should never have brought you here. Will you forgive me?"

"Always, sir."

Leonhard picked up his bow and fired at the first soldier to emerge onto the pier. The arrow found a weak spot in the armour near the armpit and the helpless elf fell immediately into the water. He stood, feeling it appropriate to give a little salute to the man who had taught him so much.

"Thank you for everything, sir."

"The honour was all mine." He turned and surveyed Herr Gareth's troops, his face as hard as granite. "Now get out of here!"

Ella and Finn rowed hard, whilst Leonhard notched as many arrows as he physically could. At first, the arrows found their targets with an incredible accuracy. But as the boat travelled further away from the wharf, Leonhard's weapon became increasingly ineffective. Herr Gareth had sensed an onslaught and had ordered half of his troops back inside the palace to pursue them on the far side of the river bank. He ordered his remaining troops to charge at General Martine.

"He's surrounded!" Finn said. "We should row back!"

Leonhard defeatedly shook his head in response. "That's what Herr Gareth wants us to do, Finn. There's nothing we can do for the General now. We must keep going!"

The dark silhouette of the palace stood out boldly against the night sky, shrouding it's serene beauty. Martine and the rest of the elven soldiers took on the forms of moving shadows with their features almost unrecognisable to the three young mercenaries watching from the boat.

The fight was over before it had begun. Martine had sliced through the first charge like a man possessed, moving with a swiftness that wouldn't look out of place for a man half his age. Herr Gareth's troops had also brought bows to the fight and he ordered them to fire. The General attempted to block with his sword, but in reality, didn't stand a chance.

A swarm of arrows pierced his chest, dropping him to his knees. His beloved top hat tumbled off his head and sank beneath the depths of the river. Almost mockingly, Herr Gareth fired the final arrow at Martine from close range and kicked his helpless body into the water.

Leonhard closed his eyes in dismay and seized Ella's hand. He looked up at the palace with a raging fury. Murder had been committed this night. The bells would ring out in the morning, proclaiming the death of the King. He wondered what lies Davini would tell Ilsthyr's citizens. Would they actually believe it?

Leonhard clenched his fists together, knowing that she was up there, somewhere. Maybe she was looking down at them right now.

'You have taken away two people that I care about and framed my father for a murder he didn't commit,' he brooded. *'I swear that one day you will get what you deserve!'*

He picked up the third oar and between Finn's sobs, the three mercenaries rowed on hastily in silence.

Eighteen

The dwarves had been ready for the Focean army as they reached the base of the Morodir mountains. Rufus Salt had heard of the little fighters fearsome reputation in battle, but he had been astounded how quickly they were set upon under a fierce storm of rain, white hail and thunder. The dwarven soldiers had used the terrain to their advantage, attacking from above as the Foceans pressed up the mountain through the abundance of narrow passages. A large number of Salt's army had their heads caved in before they had time to aim their rifles at their attackers. The captain knew then that the battle could well and truly be lost before they reached the gates of Kahr Dovidor.

"Listen up everybody!" Salt cried against the howling winds. "For every man moving forward, I want another directly behind scouting for what is above. Have your weapons ready to fire at once!"

It was at that moment that a ugly looking dwarven woman leapt down, attempting to hack at Salt's legs with a dull mace. Braced against his shoulder, Salt struck the dwarf with the base of his rifle. He then spun the weapon around with breakneck speed and fired it straight into the woman's face.

As his army moved forward once more, Salt called Salamander over for a word. "I see no rifle on you, Ser. May I ask where it is?"

"I was fed up of hearing night after night how Ser Belsay had jammed his rifle during the Battle of Sleima," Salamander said. "So I gave him mine, Captain."

"You misunderstood me. I paid a lot of money into the development and research of those weapons so my army could be the greatest force the world has ever seen. I specifically instructed every soldier to proudly carry his rifle into battle. That includes you, Ser Salamander!"

He paid no heed to Salt's protestations, holding out his cobalt coloured sword instead. It was a small, yet beautiful thing. The blade shone like a gemstone in the gloom. Salamander had snuck out one night from the Northwood orphanage he was living in after his parents had died and stolen it from the weapon shop in town. It had been at his side ever since. Therefore, the rifle had simply felt peculiar in his hands.

"Look around you, captain," he said, pointing to the fallen Foceans littering the tunnel. "Your rifles are not much use in closed quarters. A sword will do me just fine."

Salt remained impassive and seized a weapon from a nearby fallen soldier. "I am not asking, Ser," he said, pushing the rifle into Salamander's midriff. "I am ordering you to use one!"

Salamander flung the rifle over his shoulder and carried on up the mountain. He received a gash on his left arm from a stray bullet and his feet had given away on the icy tracks on a couple of occasions. Yet, it encouraged him to see he was in a finer shape than the majority of the sodden survivors.

In the open field, the rifles did actually becamne a lot more effective. The Foceans simply massacred the charging dwarven army and the archers on the walls with heavy gunfire. The dwarves' defensive resolve disappeared altogether as their King lay face down in the dirt with multiple bullet wounds to the head. The surviving dwarves soon fled towards the other settlements in the mountain range, leaving Salt with a clear route ahead.

Walking through an immense stone pergola and into the mountain itself, the vast city of Kahr Dovidor opened out before them, with the upper levels connected to the surface by a vast network of shafts and tunnels.

Twirling his moustache, General Felix surveyed the gaping drop below them.

"According to our maps," he said, unrolling the parchment, "the chamber we are looking for should be…erm…there!" He pointed it out to Salt, who squinted into the distance.

"You have better eyesight than me, Felix," Salt said. "I will take your word for it."

As they ventured further below, bioluminescent plants radiated the corridors in a deep yellow glow, replacing the natural light levels from the surface. Miniature tunnels had been crafted out of the rock, leading to the living quarters of the city. Salamander was startled to catch sight of a large farming area in the distance, home to various species of fungi and a subterranean lake with leaping fish. He hadn't given any previous thought to how self-sufficient the dwarves would have been and had expected the city to be chaotic and disorganised, which was actually far from the truth.

The mines and forges were located far below the surface, with the temperature swelteringly high. Streams of simmering magma flowed through rigid tunnels, designed with reinforced grates. Miniature minecarts loaded with piles of coal, shovels and hammers sat on the crest of the tunnels, looking forlorn and abandoned with no dwarves around to operate them. Salamander felt the rainwater evaporate from his uniform at once, with his undershirt sticking to his skin like glue. His mouth became increasingly dry and he, like many others, took on water to keep hydrated in the intense heat.

"How much further, Felix?" Salt asked, short of breath. To Salamander, it was good to know even the Captain was struggling in this climate, under his thick black attire.

"Not far, Captain. According to the maps, the entrance to the vault should be directly below us. We can use one of these mining tunnels to access it."

"Which one, goddammit? There's too many to choose from."

Salt was right. Hundreds of holes had been drilled into the rockface that mimicked the inside of a wasps nest.

"It must be this one!" Felix said, leaning next to the largest shaft.

"How can you be so sure?"

"An educated guess, Captain. Allow me to explain; there are no tracks in front of this tunnel, whereas the others are well worn through heavy mining use."

"That is true," Salt said, sounding only partially convinced.

"Also, this must be the tallest shaft for a reason. Large enough for, let's say, a certain fire guardian to pass through."

"You better be right about this Felix. My patience is already wearing thin. Otherwise, you will be spending the rest of your days locked in the vault with only your beloved maps for company."

It turned out that General Felix was indeed right. Standing before the towering metal gates, Salamander rubbed at his stinging eyes and helped his comrades prize the doorway open. He felt a flood of intense heat pass over his head and gulped as he saw what waited for them inside.

The cavern was filled with steaming magma, with only a small path to travel across. It narrowed further as it ventured towards a lava pond, where a sleeping beast guarded a floating, scarlet coloured crystal.

Leaving the Sorceress behind at the Godeburg Academy to rest, Salt had informed Salamander of the plan to retrieve the fire crystal and utilise its power. At the time, Salamander had thought the mission crazy. Standing before it now, it seemed wrong to doubt the man.

After receiving no volunteers to go first, Salt picked out twenty men to follow him and General Felix in, ordering the rest of his depleted forces into an orderly formation in case the guardian broke through.

"Ser Salamander," he shouted, "you're up!"

"I am?" Salamander didn't know what was worse; being in Sleima's throne room with the rotting Sorceress or here, waiting to be crushed by the guardian. "And just how are we going to get past that monster?"

"Don't you worry about that, Ser. All I need you for is to protect me when the time comes. It's time to see how good you really are."

"And the magma?"

"Yes indeed. Make sure you don't fall in."

Salamander felt every eye on him. If he attempted to walk away now, he would be shot doing so and go down in history as a coward and a deserter. He had gone too far to give up now.

The unsightly beast, deep brown in colour with a bright red ruff and razor sharp horns, remained dormant as the troops crept nearer. Its deep snores sent ripples through the fiery lake either side of the pathway. Each man watched their feet with intent, knowing that one misstep would end in certain death.

Salamander wiped at his brow and glanced behind him. Rufus Salt had stayed at the gates, watching General Felix lead his men towards the crystal. A strange gold object glinted in his palms.

"Keep going, Ser," a Focean soldier whispered at Salamander. His jaw trembled as he spoke and he was pale even in the volcanic light. "The General is waiting for us."

Felix had stopped a short distance from the beast and had his rifle ready. He made a strange gesture towards Salt and the shrill notes of a harmonica opened the eyes of the beast.

We are too close,' Salamander thought, taking a step back. The men behind him did the same, fearful of what might come next.

"Have your weapons at the ready!" Felix cried. "Aim for its head! Do not under any circumstances hit the crystal."

The beast awoke and instantly leapt onto all fours, roaring with fury until its throat was raw. It's red eyes flicked in confusion between Salt at the back of its lair and the men directly ahead. The tune Salt played became as haunting as a funeral march.

Bullets rang out towards the guardian's vital parts, filling the air with the smell of sulphur. The beast stumbled vigorously, but threw itself in defiance towards the source of the music. Felix and the men nearest to him never stood a chance. It swept them aside into the fiery pits as if they were nothing more than bothersome flies.

The rank of soldiers then broke, fleeing towards the exit. Salamander trailed, hearing the guardian hot on his heels. He stopped at Salt's side and took heed of the man. The captain started to play the harmonica with more urgency, but still carried on regardless.

What is he doing!? This is no time to be playing music!'

Salamander gaped again at the beast. It's movements were noticeably slower and it now tottered down the path in a languid daze. The tune was actually sending it to sleep! Through the slit in the veil, Salt considered the rifle strapped on Salamander's shoulder.

Salamander was locked in a quandary. Should he flee like his comrades or stay and bravely defend the Captain? He spun around and held the rifle out, his fingers trembling on the trigger. He aimed it upwards at the beast's head and missed the target.

'What am I doing? Would Salt do the same if the positions were reversed?'

He thought not. Still, the mission had been to retrieve the fire crystal and to do that, someone needed to be brave and kill the brute that guarded it.

Salamander went on one knee and aimed again. He shook like a leaf as the guardian inched ever closer. Three more steps and it would be on them both. It had to be now or never.

He aimed the rifle once more. It seemed to weigh a ton in his hands. He sucked in a deep breath and closed his eyes.

Two steps. All sounds, including Salt's harmonica, faded in his head.

One step. Letting his previous doubts melt away from his consciousness, he squeezed the trigger.

The bullet whistled in the air, travelling at fifteen hundred miles per hour. It hit the beast squarely between the eyes. It fell forward, sending massive plumes of dust shooting around the pair.

At once, Salt withdrew the harmonica and pulled Salamander to his feet. He said nothing to him, nodding only once and turned back towards the cave entrance.

"Yeah, you're welcome, Captain!" Salamander shouted, conveying contempt.

He returned to find Salt and the rest of the army surrounding a dishevelled man in chains. The man's matted beard came down to his chest and he wore an oversized grey jumper that was covered in black dirt. It was only as Salamander got closer that he recognized him to be an elf.

"We found him hiding in the tunnels, Cap'n," a soldier declared.

"Well, well, well, Ruven Solveig!" Salt said surprised, lifting the elf's chin with a finger. "You're a long way from home, aren't you? I've been looking for you."

"Do I know you?" Ruven asked bitterly.

"You should. We travelled north together once."

It was then that Salt lifted his mask away to reveal himself.

"Rufus! How is this even possible?" Ruven felt the shock as if he had been slapped. "Me and Francis saw your body. You were dead with a hole in your stomach!"

Salt took his leather coat off and lifted up his undershirt, showing him a deep knotted scar around his abdomen.

"Remember that healing pool, my old friend? I had enough life in me to crawl into it and feel it work its magic."

"This is impossible!" Ruven's eyes suddenly bulged with dread. "Wait, if it revived you, that means…please do not tell me you brought my sister back?"

"The Sorceress is alive, but she is weak. It has taken years of patience to get to this moment. But now we have you, we can restore her to her full power."

"No, Rufus! Please do not do this! You are making a huge mistake!"

"Take him away," Salt said, throwing the order to the nearest soldier. "Everyone else, get back in there and retrieve the crystal! We got what we came for. We will leave for Godeburg Academy at once!"

The adventure continues with 'The Unrivalled Power,' the thrilling next part in 'The Bringer of Shadows' trilogy!

COMING SOON...

Printed in Great Britain
by Amazon

75824161R00142